Sometimes it's good to miss a bus. It might be the wrong bus.

STEVE GUTTENBERG

Contents

Foreword

This story is set in the area of Inverness. Although incorporating known cities, towns and villages, note that all events, persons and specific places are fictional and not to be confused with actual buildings and structures which have been used as an inspirational canvas to tell a completely fictional story.

Acknowledgement

To Susan, Jean and Rosemary for your work in bringing this novel to completion, your time and effort is deeply appreciated.

Novels by G R Jordan

The Highlands and Islands Detective series (Crime)

1. Water's Edge
2. The Bothy
3. The Horror Weekend
4. The Small Ferry
5. Dead at Third Man
6. The Pirate Club
7. A Personal Agenda
8. A Just Punishment
9. The Numerous Deaths of Santa Claus
10. Our Gated Community
11. The Satchel
12. Culhwch Alpha
13. Fair Market Value
14. The Coach Bomber
15. The Culling at Singing Sands

Kirsten Stewart Thrillers (Thriller)

1. A Shot at Democracy
2. The Hunted Child

The Contessa Munroe Mysteries (Cozy Mystery)

1. Corpse Reviver
2. Frostbite
3. Cobra's Fang

The Patrick Smythe Series (Crime)

1. The Disappearance of Russell Hadleigh
2. The Graves of Calgary Bay
3. The Fairy Pools Gathering

Austerley & Kirkgordon Series (Fantasy)

1. Crescendo!
2. The Darkness at Dillingham
3. Dagon's Revenge
4. Ship of Doom

Supernatural and Elder Threat Assessment Agency (SETAA) Series (Fantasy)

1. Scarlett O'Meara: Beastmaster

Island Adventures Series (Cosy Fantasy Adventure)

1. Surface Tensions

Dark Wen Series (Horror Fantasy)

1. The Blasphemous Welcome
2. The Demon's Chalice

Chapter 1

Alison waved at Dougie sitting in the front seat of the bus. It would be Dougie's rotation now, and if she was quick, she could grab a lift. But had he seen her? Yes, there he was, waving back, telling her to hurry up.

Alison Cabbage had finished her rotation on the buses and was now heading for home. As per usual, she was trying to grab a lift on company transport to get there, having not brought the car into work. It was too hard to park, the station being stuck in the middle of the city centre. Everywhere you went, you had to pay extra, even in those big multi-stories. If only the company had a car park, but then again, it would be a bit off, a bus company trying to get their employees to all take the car into work. Better advert for their drivers to grab the bus. On the bright side, at least, you got to travel for free.

Alison lived just before the airport in a small cottage. It wasn't near a bus stop, but when you knew the drivers, it was easy enough to get dropped off. Her house was at a junction, so these large coaches could pull over at the small slipway, drop her off and re-join the main traffic flow without any hassle. She would then stand and watch the bus as it took the roundabout for the airport turnoff, some five hundred metres

1

ahead. She enjoyed the buses, loved her job, and was now happy here, up in Inverness.

Alison had tried a relationship once, even got to the point of being married, but it had fallen apart. She was unsure whether it was his fault or hers. Ultimately, it didn't matter because they didn't get on, but she decided to return to her maiden name of Cabbage. After all, she married a man called Mr. Onions. Sometimes, life just felt like a comedy. After all, cabbage and onions always went well together, didn't they? Apparently not.

The coach doors slid open, and Alison jumped up the two steps and slid into the seat across from the driver. Dougie gave her a nod but said nothing else as he closed his doors, put foot to the floor, and the bus started to make its way out from the enclosed station.

The bus station was comprised of several ranks that buses held at, awaiting their customers, each rank being a small platform, paved, with bus shelters on them. It was a type of road sidings, similar to a train network, but the bus station was also hidden away behind the train station, and the buses had hard manoeuvres to get onto the city centre streets. From there, they made their way back out to the more expansive roads that ran around the edge of the city of Inverness.

This was the airport bus, and it would only stop a few times on the way out to the single terminal. Most people onboard would be going to the airport with luggage safely stowed away underneath. However, like Alison, there was usually a small smattering of people who would jump off at various stops just beyond the A9 on the road out to the airport.

Dougie continued down the small narrow street that led out from the bus station to the city centre. He stopped at a red light. When he sat back, Alison could see him stretching his shoulders, trying to relax, but she knew he had a long shift ahead of him.

'You just started, Dougie?'

'Yeah, to and fro we go. Is that you off now?'

'Yes,' said Alison, 'that's me until the weekend. Got a couple of extra days simply because I have to. Time running out on them. They told me I had to take a holiday; otherwise, I'd lose it, so I'm taking it.'

'How'd you end up with holiday left over anyway?'

'Look I just—you know me, I like my work. Keeps me busy. I haven't really settled in to doing a lot of things up here yet, but I will. I'm getting there, Dougie.'

'I hope you're not waiting for that special passenger. The millionaire passenger that comes on, sees a woman he likes at the wheel, and sweeps her away. It doesn't happen,' said Dougie.

'It happened to you,' said Alison.

'Yes, it did. All except the millionaire bit. Joan's not really got that much money behind her. Not that I'm complaining, before you tell her. I didn't marry her for her money, and neither did she marry me for mine. It's a good job really. We can live on little because with three kids, you don't have a lot.'

Alison laughed, the light turned back to green and she kept quiet, allowing Dougie to concentrate on taking the bus out onto the main roads.

Inverness was looking splendid. There was a bright piece of sunshine that had decided to invade the city, draping the high walls of the city centre buildings in a sweet light that turned them from dark, damp brine to a deeper caramel colour, like a particularly appetizing sticky toffee pudding.

Alison looked around her as the bus made its way to the

flyover of the A9, and Dougie carefully steered, taking the bus out beyond the shopping complex, where the largest cinema in town also stood. Alison thought she might pop back later in the day to see what was on. She'd been going to films a lot on her own, and she really needed to get out of that habit. Maybe she could ask some of the people at work, or maybe down at the gym. That was another thing to kill time, wasn't it? The gym. You could go in there, run hard, build up a sweat and really not get to know anyone. At least, in work you got chatting.

She needed something more social. Maybe she'd join a book club. Go on one of these organized walks. She certainly wasn't going on online dating. No, that's where she'd found Mr. Onions. A perfect match, they'd said. They'd find the perfect mate. Well, they were wrong on that, so this time she'd do it on her own.

The advantage of sitting at the front in the bus was you got to see out of the large windows. Alison enjoyed these trips home because for once she didn't have to watch the road; instead, she would study the houses at the side, the estates up on the hill, and the other mainstays that she saw on her way home every day. Looking out to her left, she saw what she thought to be some sort of processing plant. She was never quite sure what it was, but there was smoke that came out the top of a tall chimney. Maybe it was a cement factory, something of that ilk.

The smoke was always coming out and you could tell the wind direction from it. Now, it was drifting up and maybe slightly towards the airport. Yes, this afternoon would be good. Maybe it was time to stay in the garden. Was it even warm enough to catch a few rays? Alison wasn't one for sunbathing, but if she could sit there with a nice cup of tea and maybe a decent book, she might just do that. Would a bronzed body help with the future capture of another husband?

Husband. Alison chided herself. *Who said anything about a husband? It's time to have a bit of fun. Find a guy who wants to have fun with me. Maybe it was the marriage last time that ruined it all. Maybe we should have just stayed friends, kept our own places.*

Alison looked down at her hands. There was still a white mark where her ring would've been. She'd worn it for three years after all, but it was very snug. That's what came when you didn't work out what size the woman's finger was before buying her the ring. They were going to get it adjusted, but as the arguments grew, and time went on, that didn't happen.

'This is you, Alison.'

Alison looked up, the bus coming to a halt in the slipway beside the small road that went past her house. Looking across, she saw her front door bathed in the sunshine. *Yes, this afternoon would be good.*

'Thanks, Dougie. You take care of yourself, okay.'

'Yes, we're nearly there, and then time to head back again. Only be doing this another what . . . twelve times?' Dougie laughed.

'At least, you didn't have to stop off on the way. I mean, did we stop at all?' asked Alison. It was then she realized just how involved with herself she'd been, because she hadn't talked to Dougie. No, she hadn't really clocked what had been going on.

'Yes, people have gotten off, two.'

Two different people? Anyway, what did that matter? She only needed to know those things when she was driving the bus. When she was sitting with her feet up on her way home, she could forget

5

all that. After all, she wasn't on the clock anymore. That stopped when she walked out of the bus station door.

Alison grabbed her bag, which contained the empty lunchbox that she brought in with her, waved to Dougie, and made her way down the small steps and then onto the pavement beside the main road. She stopped, turned around, and gave Dougie a smile. He was always quite friendly to her, and in a nice way, not as if he was looking for something. He was a married man after all. She looked upon him as a friend, not a close friend, not someone you would tell a lot to. Just one of those friends of the everyday who you pass the time of the day with, the sort that keep you going. People who were just genuinely decent and helpful.

In some ways, it was like a little family at the bus depot. After all, they'd all rallied round when Ian had that trouble with the heart bypass. He'd been the only provider in the family and others helped his wife get about, giving her lifts here and there. People like Alison had sent her gifts of food. Things just to make life easier. Yes, she was happy. It was a good family at the bus depot.

Alison stood watching the bus pull away, merging out into the traffic. She looked at the wing mirror because it showed Dougie's concentrating face watching the traffic ahead. The buses never pulled away quickly as it took time to build up momentum for such beasts, but once they were moving, they could hold a steady 50, 60, even a 70 on a motorway without thinking about it. Here, Dougie would only get up to a steady 40. He'd take a left at the roundabout ahead and end up at the airport. Alison had covered this route many times as well. When she first joined, that's what she had ended up doing; taking over everybody else's run as they went on holiday, but slowly she got more established. She usually would find herself heading north towards Tain these days.

Alison turned to let the sun hit her face and began her walk towards the house. Yes, the bus company life wasn't bad at all. With one last look, she smiled at the bus as it reached the roundabout to turn left.

The world shook. A thunderous explosion consumed Alison's hearing and vision as the coach seemed to rip apart. The top half was pushed off to one side, slamming into cars on the other side of the road. The coach had just reached the roundabout, and part of the vehicle seemed intact, including the front where Dougie sat, although it was on fire. The rear was also intact but the middle section had been ripped apart. Glass had shattered everywhere.

Cars arrived, screeching to a halt, and Alison began to run forward towards what was now a burning mess. Birds were flying around above her, all sent into a flurry at the loud explosion, and as she ran along the road, she saw people getting out of cars. Some reached for phones, others ran towards the burning wreckage. There was a thunderous bang as cars slammed into each other, and Alison suddenly stopped.

What was she doing? What was she going to do up there? Dougie, she thought, *Is Dougie all right?* Again, she started to run, not really knowing why. As she got closer to the coach, someone tried to hold her back, but she shoved them to one side. She heard someone say, 'Ambulance, police, bloody everything.' With the middle section of the bus having had its top blown off, Alison was able to look in and could see figures. It was like some sort of apocalypse movie, and she struggled to comprehend what she was looking at.

Off to her left was a limb, possibly a hand at the end of it.

What about Dougie? That was where her concern was. She ran up to the bus peering in through the double doors that had so recently opened to let her out. Dougie was there in the driver's seat. At least, part of him was. Above Dougie's shoulders was not there, and Alison turned to vomit on the floor. It was there that she saw more body bits beside her and she began stumbling before someone grabbed her.

'Dougie,' she shouted, 'Dougie.'

'This way, this way, love. You can't do anything. You can't do anything. We've phoned people. They're on their way. We can't do anything.'

'But Dougie, I need to get Dougie out.'

'Who's Dougie?' asked someone.

'The driver.'

'Dougie is not coming out, love. Dougie is not going anywhere.'

Alison allowed herself to be pulled back, but the heat from the fire could still be felt. She had stood so close as if nothing mattered, as if it was perfectly normal, but now the tears started to flow. *What on earth? Why? Who?* Questions raced through her mind. Questions that had no answers, and she sat down at the roadside, head in her hands, and wept.

Chapter 2

Macleod had heard the explosion sitting in Inverness police station. It hadn't rattled the windows, so he knew it was not that close. All the same, it sounded more intense than most things that occurred during Inverness's typical day. As he sat at his desk, looking through other case reports, Macleod began to wonder what the sound had been. He went to the office door, opened it, and shouted through to Clarissa Urquhart who was sitting behind her own desk.

'Any idea what that was?'

'No, Seoras,' said Clarissa. 'Certainly, quite big. Probably something at the docks has gone wrong. Something like that.'

'How are you getting on with that last case report?' asked Macleod. 'I said I wanted to see it today.'

'And today you shall see it. Just get off my back because you've run out of things to do.'

'It's never a bad thing to have nothing to do in this job. It means people are safe.'

'Or other people are just getting away with it, and we're none the wiser.'

Macleod looked at Clarissa and then saw the wry smile

behind her terse face. She hadn't been with the team long. Frankly, Macleod admired the work that she did although she was, at times, a little bit too feisty for him. She'd come into her role as a junior to detective Sergeant Hope McGrath but Macleod was finding it hard to see Clarissa in that position. Clarissa was a more mature woman, her years heading towards those of Macleod's, and she was eccentric. Even today, she sat in the office, a pink scarf around her neck and a jacket that looked more at home on the *Antiques Roadshow* than it did on a police officer.

The door to the investigation team's office flew open and Ross ran inside.

'There's been a bomb, Inspector, a bomb. It's blown a coach apart up at the airport.'

Detective Constable Allen Ross was out of breath having just scrambled up three flights of stairs in an effort to tell his boss what had just happened in the outskirts of Inverness.

'A bomb? Really, Ross, somebody's blown up a coach?'

'That's a bit unusual, isn't it?' asked Clarissa.

'Well, somebody once blew up the Skye Bridge, but he kind of had form.'

Macleod shot a look at Ross before turning around to grab his coat and hat from inside his own office.

'Get McGrath. Tell her to meet us on the way there. How long ago did this happen?'

'Did you not hear it, sir?' asked Ross.

'Yes. I heard it, but that was a while ago. How long has it been?'

'Twenty-five, thirty minutes maybe.'

'Right. We'll be going into a hot scene then,' said Macleod. 'We stay back, let the first responders deal with what's there, then we start picking things up. Anybody spoken to Jona?'

Jona Nakamura was the senior forensic lead at the Inverness police station and would no doubt have her work cut out over the next twenty-four hours.

'No, sir. I'll get her,' said Ross running back out of the room. It was then that Macleod noticed Clarissa hadn't moved off her seat.

'Are you okay, Sergeant? Time to shift.'

'A coach, Seoras, a whole coach. Are there many dead?'

'I don't know who's dead, I don't know what we're going to see, but yes, it's probably going to be bloody, and there's probably going to be a lot of bodies lying around, but we need to get going.'

Clarissa raised herself slowly to her feet. Almost absent-mindedly, she made her way over to grab her large coat, where it was hanging at the wall, and put it on.

'How many do you think they'll be, Seoras?'

'What's a bus hold? Fifty? Could be up to around fifty casualties. Of course, if it's going off while the bus is on the road, you could have cars here, there, and everywhere. Could be other accidental injuries rather than just the targeted.'

'It was definitely a bomb?'

'Now that's a thought,' said Macleod. 'We don't want to go too quick into this. We need to get out there, stay back, look around what's happened, and then once we've got everybody clear and dealt with, we take charge of the scene.'

'A bomb,' said Clarissa again, clearly still struggling with the concept. 'Terrorists?'

'No, no,' said Macleod. 'Don't go there. We've got a potential bomb. We've got a bus and a lot of dead people. I've got enough problems here trying to unscramble the thoughts in my head on how we're going to run this. I don't need people making unwarranted allegations.'

'I wasn't making the . . . no, I wasn't. It's just, well—'

'Switch on, Sergeant, come on. Let's get going. When you get there, you treat it like every other crime scene. You're going to see things you don't want to see, but we're in the murder team. That happens. Hold yourself together, shove it to the back of your brain, deal with what's in front of you. Okay?'

Clarissa nodded, finding her pocket for her car keys, and then looked up at Macleod.

'Let's go then.'

Macleod raced to the car and found Hope waiting. She was dressed, as ever, in her black jeans, leather jacket, but instead of her usual welcoming smile, she wore a grimace.

'Word on the street is it's definitely a bomb.'

'I'm not interested in the word on the street,' said Macleod. 'We get there, we do this thoroughly. Ross is getting Jona, Hope. Uniform is going to be all over it. I'll take overall charge, but you're taking the scene,' said Macleod as he slid into the car. 'Cover your bases, make sure all the evidence is picked up, everything's not contaminated. Watch out for Clarissa. She's already a bit shocked from this. I'm not sure if she's seen something like it.'

Macleod's mind was on overtime, scrambling through ideas and thoughts about how best to handle this. 'We'll need to get information off the bus company. See how many people were on. Wonder which bus it was. If it's a short run out towards the airport, they're not going to have booked it. There's just going to be people on.'

'Hell, sir. That's going to be a nightmare.'

'Yes, it is. You're going to have to think CCTV. You're going to have to look at the bus station, see who was getting on. That's a point. Something for Ross to do. Also, make sure he's got plenty of backup on this. There's going to be so much information to go through. But first things first, let's get there, get on the scene, control it.'

Hope nodded and the car pulled away, followed by several police cars and Jona in her smaller forensic vehicle. The traffic was already reaching gridlock proportions as Hope tried to exit out onto the A9 amidst the stuck vehicles, her flashing blue light slapped on top of the car's roof. Slowly but surely, they made their way along to the main flyover that headed out towards the airport. Traffic was already backing up from where the explosion had taken place. One of the vehicles caught in the jam was a TV camera crew with a conspicuous satellite dish on top of the car.

'And that's something else,' said Macleod, 'they're going to be all over this. We're going to have to keep it tight, keep away from them, keep all thoughts in with ourselves. It's no-comment country.'

'It's always no-comment country with you, anyway. When did you ever deal with the media well?'

Macleod tossed a glance over. 'That's not helpful at a time like this.'

'No. I'll deal with them if you want though.'

'No, you won't,' said Macleod picking up his mobile; 'besides, I'm calling the DCI, make sure I've got jurisdiction to take over.'

'You think he won't? He's going to give it to some sort of hotshot coming up?'

'No, he may want an old warhorse on this one,' said Macleod. 'Somebody dogged, who's seen it all before, and they can take on the rubbish that's going to come with it.'

'You're always seen as somebody who gets things done, solves the crime.'

'No,' said Macleod, 'it's because he'll want somebody that's not going to take any nonsense. That's the trouble with these sorts of things. Every man and his dog will start to get a piece of this. So, we'll work together and I'll fight off the glory hunters. You control what's happening, Hope, underneath. Get a hold of it. I'll cover you from above.'

'Of course, Seoras.' Hope continued to drive the car up the hard shoulder, and then when that disappeared, she followed a group of police officers who were splitting the cars wide. Meanwhile, the central part of the road was being used as a thoroughfare for emergency vehicles.

'Detective Chief Inspector,' said Macleod to the man at the end of his mobile phone. 'This is DI Macleod. I'm on the way to the bomb site, sir. I'm looking to take charge. Are you happy for me to run it?'

'Yes, yes. Good to have somebody there, Macleod. Just settle it down, once they got all the necessaries out of the way, okay? Just get on top of it, stabilize the whole thing. Look after it.'

'I'll update you when I'm there, sir.'

'Seoras, Keep a lid on it. I don't want this getting out of hand.'

'Yes, George. I'll do that.' Macleod hung up the phone.

'So, you're in charge then?' said Hope.

'Get on top of it. Do the necessaries. Did you ever hear the like of it?' asked Macleod.

'Just be nice to him,' said Hope; 'he might even cover the media for you.'

'No, he won't,' said Macleod. 'He knows they're going to be hungry on this one. This isn't some jolly. If there's terrorism involved, this is going to go nuts. Keep it by the book.'

'Always by the book anyway, isn't it?' She gave a smile.

When they eventually arrived at the scene, Hope had to park up half a mile away. In his long black trench coat, Macleod made his way forward before approaching a police sergeant with a bib on him indicating he was the incident commander at the scene.

'How are we going?' asked Macleod.

'Detective Inspector, I take it you're here for what's left behind?'

'Yes, Sergeant. Do you need any other assistance before I take over?'

'I still have got some casualties needing assistance. If any of your guys are first aid trained, report to our main doctor up ahead. He's looking for someone to sit with certain triage patients. We're moving them out best we can, but you can see the congestion both ways. Also, I've been taking phone calls from the flipping airport complaining about passengers not able to get in.'

'If I didn't have anything else to do, I'd take that phone call, and I'd ram it down their throat,' said Macleod. 'Anyway, I'm not being of use to you. Clarissa, Ross,' shouted Macleod back down the road, where his sergeant and constable were rapidly making their way towards the scene. 'The doctor up ahead, report to him. First job: sit beside triage patients. Keep it together, don't get overinvolved. Wrap them up, put them in the ambulance, and send them away. Then come back to me, please.' Macleod watched his team nod, not even hesitating, as they made their way forward.

'How well is the scene sealed off, Sergeant?' asked Macleod.

'I've got units out along the road, but you know what it's like at the moment. They're trampling all over this until we get everybody cleared and treated. I'll seal it off properly then.'

'Any other way around here?'

'No. Big detours. To get to the airport, we're going to have to use the side road that's further back. I've been getting the crew to do that, but we're going to have to turn cars around. I'm not doing that until I get everybody out of here, all the ambulances clear.'

'Good. Anything else?'

'Should have it for you probably in about an hour,' said the man. 'Until then, there's a media crew over there, who are getting gradually closer and closer. Can you pull some rank, jump all over them, and get them out of here?'

Macleod spun around and saw the camera crew creeping their way through the edge of the police cordon. There was also an interviewer, who was now in front of the camera, talking away, clearly, about the incident going on behind her.

'I'm on it,' said Macleod.

'You should've offered me the chance,' said Hope.

'No. You're with the sergeant here. You'll take the reins over from him, so make sure the scene is secure. As I said, I'm running top cover, and I'm going to go and do that now. Excuse me.'

Macleod strode away. *Vultures*, he thought, *always the vultures*. As he approached the camera crew, he walked up behind the woman on the microphone, who at the indication of her cameraman, turned around to see Macleod approaching.

'Detective Inspector, good of you to come over to speak to us. I'm looking for an update on what's happening.'

'The update is you shouldn't be here. This is a live scene, we've got people in serious condition, and we need to get ambulances to them, and get them away to hospital. This is a live scene; get further back down that road.'

'Inspector, we are the press; we have a right to be here.'

'You have a right to hand over that camera,' said Macleod, 'because I'm going to need it for evidence of footage of what's been going on here. Kindly keep that tape for me and get your backside down that road.'

The woman looked deeply offended but continued to put the mic forward. 'I have to warn you, we are live,' said the woman.

Macleod felt his heart beat. It suddenly quickened, but who cared. He was into it now; he was going to have to follow through.

'I don't care if you're live. I have a job to do, you're in the way, get down the road. When things are cleared up, we'll be able to give you a proper comment. Do not expect that for at least two to three hours. There's obviously been an explosion, there's obviously been a coach at the centre of it. You can see that from here. You don't need me to tell you that. Tell that to everybody at home. Traffic's going to be chaos for a while. We're sorting it and dealing with it, but we've got people to get in ambulances to a hospital. I need you to move.'

The woman stood firm, bringing the mic back to herself. 'Who do you think is responsible for this?'

'You will move,' said Macleod. 'If you do not, I shall have to take some of my highly occupied police officers and have them move someone who's causing an obstruction on a scene of crime. Now, kindly move. Next time I'm not asking.'

The woman backed down, but only because the cameraman pleaded with her to do so.

'Andrea White, I'll be speaking to you later, Detective Inspector; you can promise me that much.'

Macleod shook his head as he watched the woman go and then turned around and surveyed the scene himself. There were bodies covered by sheets in the centre of the road.

Nothing would be moved and the officers were being as careful as they could in the middle of this melee, to preserve the scene of crime. But life had to be dealt with first, those who might make it, even those who might not. Surveying the scene, Macleod thought there could be at least forty on that bus. He saw the cars that had crashed afterwards, one of which had a driver who now had a cover over his face.

Macleod had never been to war, but he wondered if you ever got used to something like this. There was the dumbfoundedness of people standing around contrasting with the practiced professionals, paramedics, and doctors in full flow of patient care. A sense of pride swept through him as he watched people he knew from the station tending to the wounded, shepherding the fortunate away, and maintaining some sense of order in an eruption of chaos.

Macleod saw Hope talking with the police sergeant running the scene. He scanned across and saw Clarissa Urquhart's face which was pure white as she helped someone over to an ambulance. *This is all just going to get more and more messy*, he thought.

Chapter 3

Macleod looked out of the window of the mobile incident unit and tried hard to see beyond the carnage that was facing him. He was trying to watch his officers, see how they were reacting. It was always important during an incident like this to make sure your team were supported. Even though they had to get on with dealing with some of the most horrific scenes that they would come across in their careers, being in the murder squad didn't make them immune to what happened to people, and deep down inside, Macleod was feeling sick to the core.

There was a rap on the door, and a young PC entered, carrying a cup of coffee.

'I hope that's how you like it, sir.'

'Thank you,' said Macleod, 'but what I said before, it's not sir. Inspector will do; Seoras, if you will.'

'Of course, Inspector.' The PC left the room. Macleod always wondered how the rest of the force saw him. At times, he felt there was a fear of approaching him and the young man who had just left the room highlighted the point. He was never cosy to work with, always challenging. That was something he never wanted to change, but sometimes he felt he could be a jovial boss, the one who could inspire, cajole his team along. His time with Hope had been rough on occasions, but she was better for it, he thought. She could stand up, deal with anyone, and she was certainly turning into the type of detective he admired.

Clarissa joining the team was a major boost. Hope, at last, had a female figure on the team that would give a prime example of how to handle anyone around her. Macleod hoped that at some point McGrath would speak to her, get closer, even though McGrath was technically Clarissa's boss. That was up to them. Sometimes you could only put the pawns in place and then watch to see how they developed.

Macleod picked up his mobile and made a call home to Jane, his partner. As often happened when incidents took off, he was late in explaining to her why he wouldn't be there that night, why he was going to be busy, and was more than simply delayed. Jane was far too used to the fact that she would receive a call after he'd been AWOL for some six to seven hours. Indeed, several times she'd phone the station just to see if he was out on a job. Of course, they never told her anything much, but at least, it put her mind at rest. Now, as the phone rang, he knew she would probably guess what was up.

'Seoras, it's about time. I was wondering when you were going to make the call.'

'Sorry, it's pretty busy here.'

'I take it you're out on the bombing,' said Jane. 'It's all over the news. They're saying a famous pop star might have been on board.'

Macleod wondered what this was all about for he had no reports of any pop star being on board. Nobody had come forward to say so. They were still trying to identify the passengers. Ross had been sent off to collect the incoming evidence, pick up CCTV footage to work out who was on the bus. Hope was overseeing that side of it as well, and Clarissa had been sent to investigate the threats, if indeed there had been any, made against the bus company.

'Pop star? What pop star?' asked Macleod.

'Sasha, you must have heard of her. She's never off the telly, Seoras.'

'No, no idea what you're talking about. You know I can't tell any of these ones from the others.'

'Well, you better find out because they're going to be coming at you, asking about it. The press, that is.'

'Well, you know I don't bother with press; they can go hang. I've got a mass murder to deal with.'

'That's all right,' said Jane, 'but I can see them on the telly now. They're right at the edge of your cordon or whatever you call it, demanding things.'

'I'm sorry?' said Macleod. 'Where?'

'At the edge of your cordon; it's live on TV. I actually saw you earlier in the background.'

'We need to get that perimeter moved back. If they can see me, they might be able to see further in. They put a no-fly zone over the top of the crash as well, which is kind of awkward considering we're beside an airport.'

'I take it there's been flight disruptions then.'

'Don't know, and don't care,' said Macleod. 'As I say, I've got work to do, so I'm sorry, love, I'm going to have to go. This will be a late one, I'll see you whenever.'

'Okay, Seoras, but are *you* all right?'

Macleod thought about giving the stereotypic answer of, 'Yes, I'm fine,' but the woman knew him too well. 'It's bad, Jane, very bad, so no, I'm not all right, but I've got a job to do, so we'll get that done first.'

'All right, love, you take care. Go get them.'

Jane always signed off like that, thought Macleod. *Go get them.* Like he was some sort of Western cowboy racing out there with a lasso in one hand, and bad men at the far end of it. He always reckoned that she had an over-romanticized view of him, despite the fact that she'd almost been thrown into an acid bath by one of the men he'd been chasing. It's funny how people saw what you did in this job; too often they saw a lot of glamour, but really, it tended to be a lot of death. There was a knock at the door and Macleod shouted for the caller to come in. The young PC was back.

'I'm sorry to disturb you, Inspector, but there's quite a bit going on at the edge. There's pop star groupies, sort of a vigil starting to take place.'

'Sasha? Is it Sasha?' asked Macleod. The young man was clearly very impressed with Macleod's knowledge of pop culture and he simply nodded.

'Where's McGrath? She's meant to be running the scene, now that the initial incident commander's gone.'

'I can't find her, sir, I think she's tied up with forensics. It's just that things are getting a little heated over there; there's a sergeant over dealing with it, but he's getting a little out of his depth.'

'I'm coming then,' said Macleod. He picked up his coffee and took a large gulp. *Pop stars.* he thought. *Pop stars, groupies; it's a crime scene.*

Macleod stormed out of the incident unit, and once clear of it, he could see what the problem was. A large number of people had converged onto the edge of the cordon and were starting to set up candles and other items as a vigil to this pop star. They also seemed to be dressed rather inappropriately for visiting a crime scene, especially one where so many people had died. There were many teenage girls, but also young women and men, possibly university students.

Macleod turned to the police constable who had asked him to attend. 'Is it me or are these people on their way to a nightclub?' asked Macleod. 'You would have thought coming to a scene like this, that they'd chosen to wear some more appropriate clothing.'

'I believe that's what Sasha wears on stage, that sort of outfit, sir. It's a trademark.' Macleod looked back and saw the bikini tops with jackets over the top. The jackets were short, cut up to the rib and very open at the front. Some of the men there were wearing similar outfits, except with a bare chest rather than a bikini top. 'I think whoever goes on stage with her dresses like the men are. She does tend to have quite a lot of male dancers around her, sir, when she's doing this.'

'Nonetheless,' said Macleod, 'this needs moved.'

'I guess that's why the sergeant wanted your diplomatic skills, sir.'

Macleod shot a glance at the PC. *Was he having a laugh at him?* The one thing Macleod was not known for was his diplomatic skills. Generally, he was seen as a grumpy, pushy sort of an inspector. Now, those who knew him well would have said something different. Macleod had every time in the world for those helping with an investigation, for those who were bringing something to the party, but for those who were in the way, his wrath was let loose.

As Macleod approached the cordon, there was lots of shouting, screaming by almost hysterical fans. He turned to the PC asking for several more officers to come over. As he approached the group, several of the young women at the front started screaming at him, asking where Sasha was, was she dead?

Macleod held up his hands, 'Quiet, let's have quiet.' There were a few more screams and Macleod held his hands up again, 'Quiet!' Behind the group, he could see several TV cameras now, all pointed on him. He thought hard to change the volley that was about to be unleashed from his mouth.

'I appreciate this is a difficult time, but as you can see, it's a difficult time for us as well. Behind me is a scene that needs to be properly investigated. That will take time. The one thing you're not going to get standing here is a quick answer. The other thing you're going to do is get in the way. We're going to move this cordon back a half mile, so please turn and walk back. If any of you have cars within a half mile area, shift them back. This is a police investigation. If necessary, and it becomes time to mourn, there will be a place for that.' Macleod didn't know where of course. 'In the meantime, I'm going to ask you to move politely. If you don't, you'll be escorted more firmly. That goes for every camera at the back of this group as well.' A young woman pushed her way to the front, accidentally shoving a teenage girl towards Macleod. She fell forward, he caught her, and she burst into tears on his arm.

'Detective Inspector, would you say there are terrorist links to this bombing?' a microphone was thrust in front of Macleod as he held the weakened girl.

'You again. I told you before, the time will come for a press conference. I said what I've said. Start moving back, and does anyone belong to this young girl in my arms?'

The reporter stepped forward again, but Macleod held his

hand up right in front of her face, 'No, it's not the time, move.' A group of girls put their hand up and Macleod saw them looking towards the friend in his arms. He gently helped her back under the cordon, and into their waiting embrace.

'I'm sorry for the wait,' he said. 'I really am, but the best thing you can do is go home. Stay together if you need to be, but we'll let people know when we know. Go home; your folks are probably worried about you. Make sure they know where you are.'

Macleod stood, watching the dispersing crowd, including the TV cameras that had to be moved on by the extra police officers he requested. He advised one of the police officers to pick up the candles and any keepsakes that were there, and simply move them back to the other end of the half mile cordon.

'Don't destroy them, don't mess about with them.' He felt like putting them in the bin. As the cordon was disappearing, he felt a tap on his shoulder, and turning round he saw Hope McGrath smiling at him. 'I think I dodged a bullet with that one,' said Hope.

'Yes, as I said, it was your scene.'

'Sorry, just in with Jona, but someone said they think Sasha is on the bus.'

'Yes, so I'm informed. I have no idea who Sasha is,' said Macleod. 'She important in some way?'

'Big star, she was a big star. If she is on, we're going to have media all over us and not the normal type; we're going to have all the entertainment ones, the ones that ask the really dumb questions.'

'Great, how are you getting on anyway?'

'Seems secure, no one is going through but forensics; no fly zone imposed; airports routing planes a different way; we've set up all the cars to travel the long way around, so everything's moving again around the city. We're as good as we can be, Seoras. Ross is off getting the CCTV and we're going to pull in later on tonight, see if we can start identifying who people are. We've gone through wallets et cetera as well, so we should have a list for you shortly.'

'How many dead?' asked Macleod.

'Last count, thirty.'

Macleod simply turned his head to look away from Hope. He felt a tear start to come to his eye. *Thirty people just gone like that.* Then, he sniffed and turned back to her.

'We need to get in order the names of these people, go and see families. No names go out to the press until we get to these families. That's important, Hope, you need to keep that tight.'

Hope should have said *I know that. Stop teaching me to suck eggs.* She didn't, she simply smiled and for that Macleod was grateful. He was going through the routine, even though he felt adrenaline rush through his body. *Thirty people,* he thought, *thirty, just like that.* Even with how used he was to brutality and murder, this was just horrific.

'Jona is going to try and work out the details regarding the bomb. They've taken residue samples. She said it was probably underneath the coach, in with the luggage. That's the suspicion at the moment, she needs to confirm that, and we need to get on to what's going on, Seoras. Why on earth did somebody blow up a coach going to Inverness Airport?'

'I don't know, Hope, but I do know we're going to have to be painstaking over this.' Macleod's face tightened as he saw a figure approach from behind McGrath. 'It's the DCI,' said Macleod. 'Get on, find Ross, and get me names. That's your priority. Good job on the scene.'

'Good luck to you,' said Hope, turning around and giving a nod to the newly arrived DCI before making her way.

'Always an impressive young lady,' said the DCI.

Macleod had worked with several DCIs in his time, but Hawkins was very old school. He'd managed to survive by being good with the media, and portraying a better image of himself, but Macleod knew him from the old days. He'd been quite a one with the ladies, and several broken marriages had him to blame. He was a good-looking chap, even now in his sixties, his face belying his age, and his body still in impressive shape. He also had a very white grin, which Macleod believed must be false teeth because nobody had a smile that perfect. What Macleod didn't like about Hawkins was he was all fluster, all image, and he got up the ranks with it.

Macleod was never about image. In fact, he was the worst image at times for the force. Instead, he was the grafter, the man who solved things. When he looked at Hope McGrath, he thought she made a terrific image for the force. He also thought she'd make a terrific officer, a true detective one day. Hawkins never would.

'Macleod, how are we doing? We're going to need to go to the press soon. They're giving us all this grief about this Sasha woman.'

'I know,' said Macleod, 'but we don't go yet. We keep it simple, short, brief details. The moment it happened, the time it happened, then we tell them we're working on it. We find the families of those who are dead, we get to them, then we do our press statement. Don't get ahead of ourselves.'

'It's easy for you to say; you should feel the heat that's coming down about this from everywhere. First Minister's been on to me about it. Is it terrorists? They want to involve others.'

'Nothing to say it's terrorist at the moment, sir,' said Macleod. 'I haven't got a lot to be able to say anything at present; we're still putting the bodies back together.'

Normally, Macleod would never make such a comment, but it was done for the man's benefit. A taunt to the man, who never got stuck in an investigation.

'Yes, well, your field. I'll do that. I'll give them a basic statement, but I'm going to need you with me when I do it. You're the face of the investigation; they know you in this town.'

'I will be there when you need me, Inspector, but for now, I have work to do. If you will excuse me.' Macleod walked off. He didn't really have a lot to do in one sense, because he didn't know where he was going yet with his investigation. His troops were out gathering the information. Clarissa was off to the bus company, and he could have gone with her, but instead, he trusted what she did. Now, he needed to sit and think on this one, needed to look for the angle of how they were going to find who did this. Macleod returned to the mobile unit, and to his coffee that was now going cold.

Chapter 4

Hope McGrath picked up the phone and dialled the number for Inverness Police Station. Once she was connected, she asked to be put through to Sergeant Allinson. She swallowed as she said the name. It wasn't that long ago that she was sat on the beach with him in a far-off sunspot hoping for a perfect time together.

The arguments started, they drifted apart, and had several acrimonious incidents together at the station. In one particular case, he questioned her competence and tried to make her be disloyal to Macleod. However, Sergeant Allinson was also the man she needed to investigate this pop star angle. Technically, she was a missing person, and as they had absolutely no indication she'd been on the coach, she didn't want to tie up her own resources.

'McGrath, or is it Hope?'

'Allinson, I've got something for you.' Hope was determined to be formal as possible.

'I thought you would be quite busy,' said Allinson. 'Macleod's overseeing that bombing, isn't he?'

'I'm right here as well, but I need your help or rather, I need you to investigate something that should be on your plate.

Missing person. Name of Sasha, the pop star.'

'Has there been a formal request?' asked Allinson.

'No, but I've had a crew of people here saying she was on this coach. I have no indication she was, but she's such a media celebrity, we need to debunk this straight away. I need you to go and find her. If she is missing, find out where she's missing.'

'She's one of those pop stars, isn't she? Is she the one with the bikinis?'

'Yes, that's her. I thought you'd like that. Oh, no. You prefer them without them, don't you?'

It was stupid and it was catty, but Hope felt such a vileness about the man that she couldn't help herself.

'Well, I have to admit she's certainly worth a look.'

'You don't change, do you?' said Hope. 'Not one bit. But as you know who she is, you've got about as much information as I have. Kindly get onto it and let me know when you find her. And if she's tied into this, feedback in quick.'

'Is this a request from Macleod?'

'It's a request from me,' said Hope. 'You don't need a request from Macleod. This is from me. Given the amount of nonsense we've got going on here, you need to jump to it or the DCI is going to be all over you.'

'Yes, that'll be the DCI. Pop star in trouble. Quick, stop the press.'

'Just get it done,' said Hope tersely, 'and you can phone me. There's no need to show up in person.'

'You used to like what you saw,' said Allinson.

'I always liked what I saw. It was what was inside. It was what went on in that little mind of yours and what you thought of me eventually. I told you what I want. Ring me when you have something.'

Hope put the phone down. He was the last person she wanted to call, but in a place such as Inverness which was certainly no London in terms of size, they were always going to bump into each other again. Thankfully, it wasn't very often. Hope made her way to one of the incident command units and opened the door to see Ross sitting down inside in front of CCTV. There were two PCs in there with him, working away and viewing various bits of footage.

'How are you doing, Ross?' asked Hope.

'Working my way through. We've got the CCTV from the bus station. It's not great, but we may be able to identify everyone from there. Jona is pulling together all the evidence from the bodies, so we'll have an idea from that about who people are as well, and we'll also have the bus CCTV. We're hoping that's going to be enough.'

'Are we able to account for how many were on it yet?' asked Hope.

'From what I can see at the station,' said Ross. 'I think two people must have got off from the count the Jona has been able to do, but she did say, and this is rather bleak, that she hasn't been able to put them all back together properly yet. We may be a body or two out. She certainly hasn't said there's a definitive count yet.'

'But we've got a definitive count of who's on the bus at the bus station?'

'Well, as best we can see it, I counted it up and I reckon there's forty on it.'

'Forty? Jona said there's thirty dead.'

'Well, she says thirty but it's maybe thirty-one, thirty-two. We've got ten who have gone by ambulance to hospital; at least four of them are critical,' said Ross. 'The count could go up higher.'

'You reckon somebody must have got off?'

'Nobody's been available to interview the ones who have gone to hospital.'

'We need to get that sorted. I'm going to message down to the officers down there as soon as someone wakes up to check who got off from where.'

'We've also got the bulletins out to the public asking about what they saw of the coach on the way out here. It's not easy going,' said Ross. 'I've got a team in the other van looking at that. The trouble is that people have seen this coach. They've seen coaches like it all the time. They've got the times mixed up. Despite the substantial public response, most of the time the sightings are of no use. It's almost too common a coach design but we'll stick at it.'

'Anybody not get on at the station though?' asked Hope.

'None I can see. We had a late arrival but they didn't put anything into the bottom'

'Into the bottom,' said Hope. 'How does that work exactly?'

'From what I can tell looking at the footage, and Clarissa will hopefully clarify when she returns from the bus company, but it seems that the bus pulls up, the driver then activates the doors at the bottom which is where all the luggage goes in, certainly all the big suitcases and then people just go up, put them in and get on the coach.'

'That means that you wouldn't have to be on the coach to plant something in there.'

'Exactly,' said Ross.

'How much footage is there of that coach? How many different cameras down at the bus station?'

'Oh, we got three or four cameras. The trouble is, they

don't always get great views. Two of them are showing the wrong side of the bus. Those that are on the correct side, you're getting obscured because there's a whole large group of passengers around there. Forensics said they're going to try and obviously put back together where all the luggage was and which one contained the bomb, but it's going to be hard work and not necessarily completely accurate.'

'Okay Ross, keep on it. Check that early footage from the coach. Just see if there's anything untoward, anybody looking shifty. Also get hold of the bus company. I want to know if there's any employees on that bus, other than the driver.'

'Why?' asked Ross.

'Because sometimes they get lifts, don't they? Sometimes they use the transport even though they're not going to the airport.'

'Well, nobody's come forward to say that they were there. I haven't had anybody yet to say they were on the bus and then go off it, so I'm finding it unlikely that it stopped that often.'

'No, it's a good point, Ross, but sometimes people don't come forward. Run it through. See if anybody is identified from the company catching a lift for me, and we'll take it from there. I'm going to go over and see Jona now, get an update on where we're at. I assume Macleod will be bringing us in soon, although that may be the early hours of the morning. I think he wants to get a real pull of everything in first.'

'Well, I'm not going anywhere,' said Ross. 'I'll be here or be in the incident room behind me.'

'And there was me going on holiday,' smiled Hope. She saw Ross try and force a smile. The situation was so bleak that the normal black humour they had didn't seem to cut it this time. Hope made her way out of the incident van and walked several hundred yards to find a larger unit. Approaching the door, she got a nod from a PC who opened the door for her. 'I believe Ms. Nakamura is inside, Sergeant. I take it that's who you're looking for.'

'Thank you,' said Hope and made her way over to Jona. She was sitting at the far end of the unit, working her way through a pile of papers, and glancing up at a computer screen.

'Where are we at?' asked Hope.

The Asian woman slid off the stool she was sitting on and stood looking up at Hope. Jona was tiny beside her, not much over five feet, and she always had to gaze up at the six-foot-three tall McGrath. They'd shared a house together for a while and looked a rather bizarre couple whenever they popped out to do shopping. Hope still had a room in the same house as Jona, but now spent most of her time at the flat of a car rental manager she'd become very close to.

'Started to get some names, so we're sending officers to addresses,' said Jona. 'That's the bleak side of it. With regards to pulling together what's going on, I'm running tests on bomb material we've found. Should have that for you shortly. Also putting together how the bomb was activated. I'm not saying for definite yet, possible timer.'

'But it definitely came from down below on the bus?'

'Definitely. Looking at the explosion, what happened, it's in the midsection as well. Most of our survivors were at the rear or at the front. Unfortunately, the driver wasn't one of them. He could have told you who got on and who got off.'

'Ross says you haven't got a final body count either.'

'No. In fact, we've got people out searching amongst the trees. Some bits and pieces were blown quite far away,' said Jona. 'Once I've got a complete scene, I'll be able to offer more on it. Macleod's called me and said that he wants to sit down in the morning—5:00 or 6:00 a.m. It's going to be a long night for me to get through, but I will be there.'

'He's left it quite long, hasn't he?'

The Asian woman nodded. 'He seems to have stepped quite far back,' said Jona with a nod. 'You're here talking to me—he's not. He seems to be letting everybody get on with it.'

'Yes, he sent Clarissa down to the bus company, expecting her back. I think that's when he wants everybody pulled in together. Did you hear about that pop star? They think she might've been on board.'

'Don't,' said Jona. 'I've had the DCI onto me as well, which is shady because you don't come at me; it comes through you. But I've heard nothing—nothing that indicates she was on.'

'Is she a particular ethnic origin?' asked Hope. 'I know she looks white on stage, but you know how things are these days.'

'I don't know her particularly well, but I assume that she was white, European, but to be frank, I haven't got that much time. I've got to work through the rest of this and get what bodies I do have identified. I'm sitting down with Ross in about four hours with his team. We're going to match up and see what he's got on reports coming through. Get more names to put to faces.'

'And we're still on about thirty dead?'

'Unless they find a few more bodies, but I think they're all related bits. So yeah, thirty dead.'

Hope shook her head, her red ponytail flicking out behind her. 'I've never seen anything like this. It's brutal,' said Hope, 'Absolutely brutal.'

'You okay?' asked Jona.

'Well, I'm all right for the moment.' Hope looked back at

Jona, saw the care in the woman's eyes and a pair of hands reached out taking Hope's.

'You're good enough for this. You can do this, but stay focused, try and let that stuff go to the back, and if you need me at any point, we'll deal with it, okay? Have you called John, by the way, to tell him you'll be late?'

Hope shook her head. 'Damn,' she said, 'I got caught up. Totally caught up running around doing this, doing that. I'll get on it.'

'He probably knows that you're involved in this,' said Jona. 'He's probably guessed, but best to let him know. It might even do you some good to talk to him.'

Hope nodded and took her leave of Jona. She made her way outside. She decided she would go and visit the perimeter, see if anyone had come forward or anyone was hanging around. Often, people who caused scenes like these came back to look at the devastation, so Hope decided she would take a walk to clear her head, but also in case somebody had made a move.

It was not that Hope had become accustomed to scenes of devastation, but rather that she had grown to accept the worst head on. Already, she had the sense of the tragedy before her being transformed into a work area. There was nothing so heart wrenching as seeing the wounded and bereaved, but once they had departed, the area took on a different aspect. She could imagine there was now a manual to go with it.

There were small yellow markers on the ground indicating significant finds. Tents lay over bodies yet to be moved and over important pieces of evidence that were not ready for transport to a laboratory or store.

Hope thought she might have begun to feel at home now, working with the gruesome sights she came across. But the truth of how many people had died was not diluted just because it was catalogued. A shiver ran down her spine, and she felt the desperate need for a piece of warmth to hang onto.

As she started to walk, she thought about Jona's words, took out her mobile, and dialled her lover's number. Right now, she felt like she could go back to John's flat, jump into bed and let him hold her, but she had work to do, so this quick conversation would need to be enough for her. As she heard his words of, 'Hello,' and, 'Thank God you're all right,' she felt a tear coming from her eye.

'I'm good. I'm good. Just working. Just wanted to let you know.'

Chapter 5

Clarissa Urquhart bustled away through a scrum of cameras and press to the front doors of the bus company building. A small line of police officers was keeping the press back, and they were not giving a lot of recognition to Clarissa as she entered. She'd only been at Inverness police station for a short time, but her style of dress and sharp retorts ensured that she was known by everyone in a very short space of time. Indeed, she even saw the fear in people's eyes when she went to sit beside them in the canteen.

None of this bothered her. Clarissa was one of those people who got on with life, doing what needed done and she was enjoying the challenge of working with Macleod. She would chivvy him up out of his rather drab appearance and stone-set ways, but she had full respect for the man, for she had seen first-hand his sharp mind and the way he worked.

Clarissa was in the foyer of the bus company, where a number of people were milling around, conversation filling the room and drowning out almost any attempt she had to communicate with anyone. A number of the people looked like company employees, some possibly relatives but she stuck her hand in the air and announced broadly,

'If everyone would stay quiet, please? I am the police.'

It wasn't a classical announcement, but it got the point over as everyone turned round and looked at her, and for a moment she smiled disarmingly.

'Sorry to intrude on what were very heated conversations but I need to see the managing director. Would he be here?'

A young girl came forward. 'Sorry,' she said. 'I'm Jeanine, and I look after his affairs, so to speak, or rather, no, not his affairs, his timetable and that. Sorry, it's just been a bit hectic, bit chaotic, hasn't it?'

'Indeed, it has,' said Clarissa, 'but I need to see your boss. If you can take me there directly.'

The girl showed Clarissa up to an office upstairs, and inside Clarissa heard much more noise. Jeanine rapped the door, but nothing was forthcoming. So, Clarissa stepped past her and thundered her fist against the door. When again nothing was said, she simply opened it, turned to thank Jeanine and marched in.

Clarissa was not overly large, but her presence dominated any room she entered. She had the look of some sort of wild auntie and she could see a questioning face from behind a large wooden desk in front of her. To the side of the man in a chair at the desk were more men in suits, a woman in sharp skirt and blouse, and a couple of other men dressed in boiler suits, presumably mechanics from the shop floor.

'I am DS Clarissa Urquhart and I need to talk to the managing director. Is that you behind the desk, sir? That would be grand, and if the rest of you could get out of the room, that would be even better.'

'I'll be with you in a moment, Sergeant,' said the man behind the desk. 'I have to talk to the insurance people first, and some of the mechanics. If you could just wait outside.'

Clarissa strolled up to the desk, leaned over it, placed her hands down on it, and stared straight at the man. 'I said I'm the police. I need to talk to you. We've just had a bomb go off in one of your coaches. I appreciate you may want to be talking to your insurance, and your mechanics, and whoever that woman is but no, you're talking to me.' Clarissa stood up, turned around and looked at everyone else. 'Leave the room, please, but don't go too far, just in case I need to talk to any of you as well.'

There was a fear to comply amongst the group, and although they grumbled, they drifted out of the room.

'Ah, that's better, isn't it?' said Clarissa. 'If you pick up the phone, Jeanine's a bit busy, but I'm sure she'll be able to bring us a couple of coffees.' The man's face shrunk back, like a tamed dog. He picked up the phone and rang his receptionist before putting it back down.

'Sorry to be so abrupt,' said Clarissa, 'but time is of the essence, and while you may have a lot of things to get in order, we have a killer to catch. I will need company records of everyone who works here, I'll need to know who was driving that bus, and I need to know anybody else who might've been on that bus as well. I also need to know if anyone has made any threats against this company. I need to know what state of solvency you're in, and I need to know it as soon as possible. So, while my coffee's arriving, if you could start the ball rolling, that'd be much appreciated. You okay if I use this office to work?'

The man stood up, clearly suffering from a bout of determination.

'Now look here,' said the man, 'you can't just come in and

demand all these things.'

Clarissa took out her warrant card and her badge and set it on the table. 'That says I can, and if you want to talk to my superior, Sergeant Hope McGrath, you can. But if she doesn't convince you, you can talk to her boss, that's DI Macleod.'

Clarissa saw the man's face at the mention of Macleod's name. 'I shall just get on to it for you,' he said.

'Full cooperation is always best,' said Clarissa. 'You've had a rough time, you've got a dead driver, you've got a family that needs to be advised of that if they haven't already.'

'We're in touch with his family.'

'Any children?' asked Clarissa, almost tenderly.

'Three,' said the man. 'Three.'

'My condolences,' said Clarissa. 'But we need to find out who did this to him. So, chop to it.' As the managing director left the room, Clarissa felt her shoulders shrink back down, a wave of energy leaving her.

Three kids, she thought. *Three kids with no dad.* She'd seen the covered body still in the driver's seat and she felt some tears start to come towards her eyes. She stuffed them back. *Put it to the back*, she told herself. *Job to do. Macleod was right, job to do.* The thing about working in the art world was that this sort of occurrence didn't happen. You didn't have to deal with this. Clarissa Urquhart was only recently part of the murder team, having worked on a previous case with them. And then Macleod had made his approach. She'd been invited by him to join her team at the departure of Kirsten Stewart. Part of her was wondering if she would regret that move?

When the managing director re-entered carrying a bundle of files, Clarissa regained herself, playing the part she knew so well, the authoritarian who expected things to happen because she was in the room.

'Here's some printed documents, details about the company solvency - we're quite fluid at the moment,' said the man, but Clarissa put a hand up and stopped him, 'My apologies, sir,' she said, 'what's your name?'

'It's David Tremaine.'

'Are you a sole owner?'

'Yes. It's my company, I'm at the top, we don't have a board yet as such. We have a team; they run the company, but it is mine and mine alone.'

'Okay,' said Clarissa, 'I will get into the company details and look at your standing, but first off, do you know anyone who would want to do this to your company?'

'Frankly, no. It's crazy to me.'

'Have you had anybody say anything about your company, made any threats towards it?'

'I won't lie to you. If you check your records, you'll find we've reported a number of attacks on coaches, but they've been small-scale stuff, eggs, scrapes down the side, punctured tires, things like that.'

'Have they come from directed threats, or are they just random attacks?'

'They've been quite directed. You may know that there are certain people in this city who like to extort money, and when our bus has been operating in certain areas, we've basically been told that we need to pay money; otherwise, things will happen to it. We've reported it when things have happened, but not like this. Everything that's been done has been small scale. In fact, the money being asked for has been small scale, really, couple of hundred a month. Though to blow somebody up for a couple of hundred a month, this doesn't make sense.'

The man slumped back in his chair.

'No, it doesn't,' said Clarissa. 'It doesn't at all. How are these threats made?'

'Generally, to drivers, somebody will get on the bus, they'll say to them, you need to pay me the fare, and they'll quote a number, tell them to pass it back to the boss and they get back off. Then, if money hasn't gone in the next day, dropped off at whatever bench or wastepaper bin they tell them to, the bus gets attacked.'

'Have you ever given in? Ever given money?'

'No,' said David, 'it's not worth it. We can't do that because it will build; they'll start with a few hundred, then it will be a grand, then it will be—but this makes no sense; this was a bomb.'

'Stay calm,' said Clarissa, 'and try and concentrate on the questions. Is there anyone within your company you think could be a target for this?'

'No, I told you, they just come in and ask for money. They've never physically hurt any of the drivers or threatened them personally.'

'You're not listening to what I'm saying. I'm asking do you know of anybody in your company, their particular profile, who would be open to being threatened in this way. Any employees with problems, financially or who have run other things, done anything?'

'Not that I'm aware of. We had one young lad who was driving for us, got caught with drugs. But he went, gone. It's been a year now.'

Clarissa nodded. 'Would you have any idea of how many people were on that bus?'

'No, we didn't have the sales data come back from it,

obviously people pay with credit card and that. We can probably chase that up, see those payments made, but other people will pay with cash. How many do you think were on it?' the man asked.

'We're thinking around forty, sir. We're also thinking thirty of them are dead. There's a lot of other people in intensive care and in the hospital, so it could get worse.'

The man stood up, nodded, and walked over to a cabinet. From inside he pulled out a large bottle of whiskey and two tumblers.

'I'd love to. I could do with one of those at the moment, but no,' said Clarissa. 'I'm on duty. But, please, as long as you don't get smashed beyond belief, feel free.'

The man dropped a shot of whiskey into the tumbler, picked it up and threw it down his neck. He then placed the tumbler down and dropped another one in before making that one follow the first one. When he went to get a third one, Clarissa coughed.

'I need you sober to answer the questions. Now is not a time to get smashed; now is the time for you to support your colleagues. Your workforce is going to be in shock, and I'll need to interview them, so please call them in. We could use your offices at the front, create a passage away from the media. I'll push the press back if I have to. I'll also need a room to interview in, and I'll need to work in here myself. I'll be here until the wee hours so I'd appreciate it if there was some coffee or something about, but if you haven't got that, we can sort it. Key thing is to get a hold of all your company and get them into the building.'

The man walked back to his chair and slumped into it. Then he leaned forward and began to cry into his hands. Clarissa stood up, made her way around the other side of the desk and put a hand on his shoulder, 'I know,' she said. 'Trust me, I know. The driver, did you know him well?'

'I think he's one of our originals, Dougie Douglas,' he said. 'What a name, but he was a good driver, never any bother from him, straight-forward family man. Came in, did his work, took his pay, went home, not a problem at all, and then somebody just blows him up.'

'Do you know the wife?' asked Clarissa,

'Yes. I met her here a couple of times on workdays.'

'I suggest that the first thing you do is tell your staff to start phoning around everyone to get them in and the next thing you do is phone his wife. I take it she's rung in already.'

'Yes, she has. Obviously, I couldn't tell her for sure about anything, but now you have.'

'We will have been out to her by now. I'll just check up on that and make sure, but as soon as we're there and have told her, I suggest you ring her. If you'll kindly get on with it, sir, I'll get to work.'

Clarissa made her way back to the other side of the desk and watched the man pick up the phone. Soon the place was a flurry of activity again. Clarissa made her way back down to brief the sergeant who was standing outside the building. Once she had him organized to take the influx of company employees arriving for interviews, she made her way back upstairs and into the Managing Director's office. The woman in the sharp skirt and blouse was there.

'Mr. Tremaine is on the phone,' the woman said, 'but I'm going to take you through all the records, show you how to access everything on this computer that you will need. I'm at your disposal for anything you require.'

Clarissa nodded. 'Thank you,' she said. 'Good to know. I do advise you this could be a long one but all the assistance is gratefully received.' Clarissa spent the next ten minutes getting a basic run down of how the computer system worked. It was about three hours later when she received a call from Macleod saying that he wanted everyone back for a meeting at five in the morning so that they could share and discuss what they'd learned.

Clarissa explained what she was doing, and then repeated that explanation to Hope McGrath when she phoned an hour later. This was the gathering, the time of bringing information together.

She thought it must be hard for Macleod at this time. Everybody was doing the spade work. It's only when he got the information that his brain would leap to action. Clarissa stood at the window of the Managing Director's office and watched as people kept coming in, employees in tears.

One man she saw was holding his company jacket, the logo before him, coming up to people shouting something. Another man, quite old in the tooth, was slowly shaking his head. Various staff grabbed each other and hugged before wiping away tears while police officers stood and sympathetically directed new arrivals to interviews. And yet, out there buses were still running, coach drivers still working and maybe wondering if they would be targeted. Their small community was now having to deal with a fear they had previously never imagined. The place was a mess, awash with sorrow, and in the midst of that, she had to keep doing her job.

Chapter 6

The dawn was rising over the Moray Firth as Macleod stood at the steps of the mobile investigation unit. In a few moments he would step inside with the senior team to discuss the case so far and as to what now needed to happen. But for the moment, he was taking time to simply stare at the sun rising. There was a dampness about the ground, a dew from the morning air and if you closed your eyes and filtered out the images you could almost imagine nothing had ever happened.

Except of course you could. There were the diesel generators running for a start, thumping away, and indicating something was amiss. The residual smell of the explosion still hung in the air, stagnated by a lacklustre wind. And then you could smell the fire within the bus, the last tinges of human flesh that was burnt.

Macleod was not feeling more hopeful. There was a funny thing that happened every time the dawn came out. The idea of a new day and a fresh start had always stuck with him, but this one has been hard. As he looked around at the various tents covering all prone bodies, he went through one of those moments when he thought about his faith, and whether or not

God was even there.

The sheer brutality of this moment symbolized by the ripping apart of the coach made him ask this being he worshiped how He could ever let it happen. He remembered the comfort he felt from decent people and tried to think of the good in the world. The orange sunrise reaching out across the sky helped soothe these concerns, but he knew he would always carry them. They were part of his faith, part of him, and because of that, he would always be challenged by the job he worked in.

'It is quite lovely, isn't it Inspector?'

Macleod turned to look at the woman standing beside him who barely reached up to his shoulder. Jona Nakamura was someone who people saw as thoroughly scientific. With Macleod, she was much deeper than that. They'd often completed meditation sessions together, talked through deep issues, both religious and secular, and he found her a great person to spar off with, someone who could challenge, but in a friendly way. The way that helps build you up, not take you down.

'Are you okay?' asked Macleod. 'It's been a pretty rough one for you.'

'The forensic team is okay. We're doing what we do. When it's all over, I'll have a look and see if they're okay again and you can ask me the question.'

'And yes, you can ask me too,' Macleod smiled. There was almost a resilience to what had happened. A wall that had been built up over the years which was used to stop the dark thoughts rushing in. Jona held a file in her hand, and she tapped it.

'I think it's time to go talk about this.'

'Yes, ma'am,' said Macleod. He turned on his heel and walked up the steps before opening the door and holding it for Jona. She smiled kindly in return. 'Just get yourself set up,' said Macleod. 'I'll be just a minute.'

Macleod continued to stand at the door awaiting the arrival of the rest of his colleagues and first greeted Hope, then Ross, before he saw a car pulling up at speed towards the police cordon. There was a clump of boots as his newest recruit to the team ran across the asphalt road surface

'Sorry, I'm a tad late, Seoras,' said Clarissa. 'I was struggling to get everything down onto the file I needed.'

'Did it go well down there?'

'I'll tell you inside,' she said. 'Let's not keep the others waiting.' With that, she brushed past him. Macleod swore he was still the senior officer, although with Clarissa you were never quite sure.

Once inside, the team sat round a table. The far wall of the unit had a small projection screen that Jona was working with. Once she sat down, Macleod stood up and addressed his people.

'First off, thank you for all your efforts so far. This jumped at us yesterday afternoon, and it was all hands to the pump, so thank you. Now we're getting to the point we're used to. The point we normally take over. With that in mind, I'm going to get Jona to run us through what happened, what she knows about it, and what she thinks she can tell us in the future. Then we'll start talking about what the rest of you have found out. Jona.' Macleod sat down, and the forensic lead made her way round to her laptop, clicking on the keyboard.

'Okay. What we know so far, thirty people are dead. We have ten in hospital. One, I don't believe is going to make it through the day. Another three are touch and go. Six should come out of this fine other than the mental scarring that's obviously going to happen. In terms of who was on the bus, we have driver Dougie Douglas. I've been able to identify his body. Unfortunately, due to the force of the explosion he was carried forward into the steering wheel which crushed his ribs, a couple of cracked bones went into his lungs. He might have survived that if his head had not been taken off by the explosion. The man didn't stand a chance. Of the rest of the bodies there, we have six or seven blown to bits, literally. We had to collect them.

'We have another twenty-three that have died because they were close to the explosion, and we also have six who survived by merely being at the rear of the bus. The other four who are in more serious condition were closer to the middle. The explosion itself,' said Jona, 'was a bomb. We believe it was done by a timer, not a remote detonation. The remains of the timer have been flung in tiny pieces, and we're trying to put it back together.

'We've tested the residues of the bomb, and it's Semtex. We also believe it's possibly come from Irish dissidents but we're working on that. Of those on the bus, I would say we've identified twenty-five, and then there's the ten in hospital. I've got five left to try and work out who they are. Identification has been carried out by various methods. Fortunately, with many of them we have had wallets, credit cards, or other identification on them. Those who were rather more violently torn apart have been more difficult to identify as some of the credit cards and wallets you would expect have been incinerated. We'll continue with our identification, and we'll also trace back the bomb, get a better link into that but in short, this was deliberate. It was planned and it's been carried out to great effect.'

'Thank you, Jona. The timer on the bomb, how accurate is that? Did the person know they were going to be at the roundabout when the bomb went off? Is the place important? Also, who planted the bomb? Were they on the bus? Did they get off the bus? Hope, Ross, how are we getting on with that?'

Hope stood up as Jona sat down and started to twiddle a pen between her fingers. 'Okay, we've been having some difficulty. The CCTV footage at the bus station only shows glimpses of people putting luggage on board. Now, Jona's managed to identify some of the people, we're trying to match the bodies with people we see on CCTV. We've got about fifteen of them, but we're still working on the others. Lots of luggage was placed in the bottom of the bus. The case that the bomb came from, we're unsure of. Jona's traced it back to possibly six or seven. Of those, we believe there were three suitcases, a couple of larger rucksacks, and one small rucksack.'

'What size holder do you need for a bomb of this capacity?' asked Macleod.

'Just a small rucksack,' said Jona, 'so any of those items could have been the delivery mechanism.'

'We know the bus stopped, or at least we believe the bus stopped twice,' said Hope. 'The first time, the person getting off is very loosely described by other cars driving about. We're having difficulty making sure we get the right bus because these buses go off three, four times an hour, but we believe somebody got off. Dark getup, possibly black jeans, certainly a hoodie. Didn't have anything on them. No bags over the shoulder, no suitcases. There was a second person got off not far from the roundabout itself. In fact, from where they got off at, you could probably see the roundabout. The person was reported by drivers who were further behind the bus. We believe it to be a female, and she was wearing a jacket, possibly the colour of the bus company.'

'Do we know of anybody from the bus company who was on that coach?' asked Macleod to Clarissa.

'It's common practice for people to jump on and grab lifts back to homes, so it is likely but there's no specific bus assigned to people. Let me have a look.' Clarissa dove down into files that she held in front of her. As she fussed through her notes, Macleod was getting impatient.

'What are you looking for?'

'Addresses. Don't disturb me,' said Clarissa. This caused eyebrows to be raised by Ross and Hope, and Macleod swore that Jona almost gave a chuckle.

'There, this is it, Seoras. There's a bus company employee who lives literally a minute from where that person got off.'

'And the person's name is?'

'Alison Cabbage. Quaint name,' said Clarissa.

'As I understand it,' said Macleod, 'nobody's actually phoned in to say they witnessed the explosion with that name, or from the bus company?'

'That's correct,' said Hope. 'We haven't had anybody come forward who said they were on the bus.'

'So,' said Macleod, 'we've got somebody who's been on the bus and got off it reasonably early on. We've got somebody else who's been on the bus and got off it later, who works for the bus company—Alison Cabbage. We need to find Alison Cabbage.'

'I'll go straight to her house,' said Clarissa, 'see if she's there. I don't think she checked in at the bus company headquarters but that roundup is still going on.'

'Why wouldn't she have phoned?' asked Ross. 'You've just seen this.'

'Shock,' said Clarissa. 'She might not be there. We might have to get a search party out for her. She could be missing.'

'Since we're winding up this meeting,' said Macleod, 'straight to it please, Clarissa.' The woman nodded her head, and then went back inside her files for a moment. Macleod sat there waiting for her to finish before beginning again.

'It's all right, Seoras, I'm listening.'

Again, there was an awkward moment where everyone else in the room looked at each other before Macleod continued. 'We need to find out where this person got off. What about CCTV footage?'

'The coach CCTV footage was destroyed, unusable,' said Ross. 'I've tried looking for CCTV and traffic cameras along that road. They're getting off at the point where there aren't any. We're working through the reports of sightings, but all we've got is, they get off the bus and we don't know where they go after that.'

'Okay. Look in the surrounding area. Think about where they can go to. Carparks, streets where they can leave a car and get on to the coach. Did they get back on a different bus? Get on the CCTV footage of other buses to see if that person gets on. They're getting off with no baggage; therefore, can they change? Probably not, so they could have been seen elsewhere.'

Ross nodded, and Clarissa popped her head up from her paperwork. 'Just so you all know, the bus company was getting hassle from a lot of lowlifes, threats. Drivers were being told that they needed to drop money off. Some sort of protection. Their buses were getting egged, broken wing mirrors. Things like that were happening, but far from this sort of level.'

'There's no way it could have escalated?' asked Macleod.

'It's a bit of a jump, Seoras,' said Clarissa. 'This is not intimidation—it's war.'

Macleod nodded. 'Okay,' he said. 'Our job now is to find that person who got off the bus; it could be our link. Also keep on at the statements from the bus station. See if we can identify who put those bags on the bus. Ross, Jona, get together, tie that up. Clarissa, go see if you can find our off-duty driver who came back.'

'Also, one other thing,' said Macleod. 'The media is shouting about this pop star. I take it there's nothing come through.'

'I'm looking at the remains and so far, I can't identify her. I've asked for dental records, but it's all private dentistry, private medicine, and it's been a nightmare trying to get anything out of them,' said Jona.

'If you need me to jump in on that, tell me,' said Macleod. 'I'm going to be tied up with the DCI for the next hour, so you know what you have to do. Clarissa, you wait behind. Everyone else, get to it.'

The team made their way out while Clarissa waited in her seat trying to put her folders together.

'You okay?' asked Macleod.

'No, about as well as you,' said Clarissa. 'It's okay. I haven't seen one like this before. I've seen murders but not this. I'll be fine, or I'll get to the end of it, and I'll get fine. Just like you. You don't have to pull me aside for special treatment.'

'I'll pull you aside if I need to. It's concern, Clarissa. The Murder Team, we look out for each other and in a big way. It doesn't have to be a coachload, it can be anything, so trust me, when I ask you if you're okay, I just want a proper answer, and thank you for giving it to me.'

'Okay,' said Clarissa. 'I'll get off then.'

'Have you eaten anything?' asked Macleod.

'No, of course I haven't, Seoras. How'd I have a chance to eat anything?' Macleod reached inside his pocket, pulled out a Mars bar, and threw it towards Clarissa, but it fell two feet short of her.

'I'm good but I'm not that good,' he said, and watched her face as she started to laugh.

'You got a wicked sense of humour inside, haven't you? You're not all serious.'

'You should meet my partner,' said Macleod, 'she says I'm a riot.'

Clarissa looked back at him intently. 'No, she doesn't,' and off she walked. She made her way out the door, and Macleod ran after her.

'What did you say in there?' he said. 'That bit where I said about the intimidation. Could it escalate? You said a bomb was like . . .'

'A war. That's instigating war; that's not threatening someone. That's not intimidation.'

'Thank you,' he said, and stood on the steps, oblivious to the fact that Clarissa was giving him the strangest of looks.

As Macleod heard her boots clop away, he looked back to the dawn that had now turned into a blue sky. *There will be sunshine today, and a lot of people to explain why they lost loved ones.* Macleod stared at the sun, still rising, and he enjoyed what warmth he could from it. *War*, he thought. *Instigating a war*. Something was rumbling through his mind.

Chapter 7

Clarissa made her way back along the road towards Inverness, walking because she realized that the house was only a short distance away. She was looking for the off-duty driver but about her were the harrowed faces of colleagues from the station. It was like no one wanted to look at each other lest you had to talk about the incident, as if not mentioning it might somehow make it go away. The trees close to the incident were still standing tall as they had always done, but Clarissa thought they seemed different, as if something were amiss, like you had left the front door ajar when leaving the house.

When she found the small road off to the side where the bus had pulled over to drop Alison Cabbage off, Clarissa noted the house set back from the road, hidden amongst the trees. She stomped along in her boots, determined to make an effort in an attempt to keep sleep at bay. She was thoroughly exhausted. From yesterday afternoon, they hadn't stopped, and her time spent down at the coach company had left her drained. It wasn't a particularly cold morning, but she felt the chill in her bones and put it down to the lack of sleep. In fact, she was putting everything down to the lack of sleep, her slight grumpiness, and the rumblings of her stomach.

When she approached the house, she went through a wooden gate to a small path that led down to a bungalow. It looked like a house for a single person—a couple at most—but there was a lack of items associated with partners. No his and hers anything, quaint notices stuck on the side of walls, things brought back from holidays away from your loved one that they didn't particularly want, but felt obliged to stick out in the garden or in the porch.

As she reached the porch of the bungalow, she looked inside to a closed door. Clarissa knocked hard. 'Alison Cabbage, I'm looking for Alison Cabbage. This is the police. Are you there, love?'

There came no reply. Clarissa walked around the bungalow, rapping on the windows, and shouting inside. She saw no one. Having seen the interior, she was more assured that this was a single person's house. There was a lack of photographs, no family up on the wall, no sweethearts held together. In fact, Clarissa would say this person might have recently ended a relationship because the lack of photographs was overwhelming, almost as if she wanted to banish memories, not have them assaulting her memory every day. Having looked through every window and realizing she couldn't see anyone, Clarissa made a quick start with the garden. It was small, neat enough, with a mown lawn, but there were no plants at the side, just some trees leading into a small forest. As Clarissa turned to leave, she heard something in the undergrowth.

'Anyone there?' asked Clarissa. 'This is the police; it's okay. If you're there, love, I'm looking for Alison Cabbage. Is that you, Alison?' Then came sobbing. Deep hard sobbing.

Clarissa pushed her way in past some trees and saw a woman doubled over on the ground. She wore the jacket of a coach driver, similar to the ones she had seen down at the company. The woman wasn't petite, quite robust in a lot of ways. Clarissa tapped her on the shoulder.

'Alison? Are you Alison Cabbage?' The woman shook and Clarissa reached down, tugged at her jacket, able to turn it towards her to see the naming label on the right-hand side. This was Alison Cabbage, and she was happy to help. Clarissa picked up her phone, dialled for an ambulance and insisted it get quickly to the house. She then took off her own jacket and wrapped it around Alison, before getting down close to her and wrapping herself up with her. The woman was starting to turn blue.

When the ambulance arrived, they quickly whisked Alison into the back and drove off for Raigmore Hospital. Clarissa advised them that this was a potential witness to the bombing, and she would radio ahead for some of the police officers who were currently down at the hospital to take up a position near the casualty on arrival. The ambulance men nodded, put the casualty in the back of the ambulance and drove off. What was it to them? Their job was to get this woman to the hospital quickly and warm her up before any serious complications set in.

She's been lucky, thought Clarissa, *for last night was not a night of cold.* Here in the highlands, it could go to minus numbers so easily, but as it was only the back end of summer, temperatures hadn't dropped drastically yet. After the ambulance had departed, Clarissa made her way back to the mobile unit and found Macleod poring over CCTV pictures. She advised him of finding their off-duty driver and he looked around the room, spying Ross in the corner.

'Ross, why don't you go down and interview her? You understand what was happening with the bus journey. Hope's tied up at the moment, going through some of the other things. You can take Clarissa with you if you want.'

'I'd rather get back down to the coach company, sir,' said Clarissa. 'Want to do a bit more digging to see if there's anything going on. I know they said it was low level, the intimidation they were getting, but we need to make sure of that.'

'Fair enough,' said Macleod. 'You're on your own, Ross. Take one of the uniforms with you if you wish, but any of the detail you get, make sure you feed it back in here straight away.'

'As always, Inspector,' said Ross, giving himself a little shake. He exited the mobile unit and found his car.

Raigmore Hospital was not uncommon to Ross. He had spent time there recovering after a gunshot wound, one that nearly ended not only his career, but also his life. Having been stuck there for a while, he now had an intimate knowledge of the entire building because as he was close to finally recovering, he made a point of walking round the building daily. Was he just being nosy or was it simply prep for the job? He wasn't sure, but he liked to say it was prep for the job. Certainly, if Macleod asked, that's what he would say.

Now as he waited for his approval to see the distressed bus driver Clarissa had found, he mentally traced the building in his mind. Every now and then he would glance along the corridor he sat in, thinking how the one his mind had currently drifted to was parallel to this, or had a stripe like that on the wall, or some other common characteristic. It kept him busy and his mind free from dwelling on the recent explosion.

Ross was generally good at dealing with trauma but one thing he understood about this situation was that it would be right up there in the public spotlight. Most of the cases they undertook were completed without a camera glaring at you. Then a chipper thought came to his mind. Here in the hospital, there were no cameras, for they would be kept outside, clear of the patients inside lest they damage anyone's recovery.

It was an hour before Ross was able to see Alison Cabbage. She was now half asleep, wrapped up in blankets, on a bed. Ross entered the room and the nurse gave him a stare, but he held up his warrant card and ID.

'I apologise but I need to talk to Alison due to the nature of the incident that she witnessed.'

'Poor girl's traumatized,' said the nurse. 'Just keeps blubbering. You might struggle, officer. By all means, but don't tax her.'

Ross made his way over to the bed, sat down on the seat beside it, and looked up at his witness. She turned, opened one eye, and stared at him briefly, before closing it again. After a minute, she opened both eyes.

'Who are you?'

'I am Detective Constable Ross with Inverness police. I'm here to speak about what you saw.'

The woman turned away. 'It's not Dougie, it's not Dougie,' she said becoming rather agitated. Ross glanced over at the nurse in the far corner of the room, who was giving him the evil eye for upsetting her patient.

'Let's not worry if it's Dougie or not,' said Ross. 'Don't talk to me about what happened then. Talk to me about what happened before. You got a lift, didn't you?'

The woman nodded and turned back to Ross with a sigh. 'Yes. I just finished work, just finished. Got on with—'

'You just got on the bus,' said Ross, 'Don't worry about that. What happened when you got on the bus?'

'Well, I was late. I was just about there. He opened the door as I sat. I was watching, half daydreaming. Then I got off, and then it went boom.'

The woman said the word like it was unknown. The emphasis on the boom and the sound of explosion was so strong that Ross was wondering was she having him on.

'No, before that,' said Ross, 'I really want to talk about before that. Lots of people got on the bus. Did you see them get on?'

'No. I was late. He opened the doors for me. Giving me a lift.'

'Did you see anybody get off?' The woman lifted her hand. Two fingers were raised to the air. 'Two people, you saw two people,' said Ross. 'Who were they?'

'That one kid, school uniform on. Got off not far, near to—yeah, near to the retail site, the shopping. Probably going to the cinema or something like that, meeting parents. Maybe about twelve.'

That's interesting, thought Ross. *Nobody else saw a school kid get off. It's funny how we miss the small people in life.*

'Anybody else?' asked Ross.

'Yes,' she said. 'Got off looking like one of them Muslim women.'

Ross rolled his eyes. He was waiting for the racist remarks, waiting to hear how the bomber was someone in a burka. 'Was she Muslim?' asked Ross.

'No, no. Like Muslim,' said the woman. 'Covered but in jeans. They had jeans, light jeans and a cover.'

61

'What sort of cover?' asked Ross. 'Do you mean like a hat?'

'No,' said the woman. 'The hat's attached to the back.'

'Like a hood?' The woman held her hands up, using a fist as if she was cheering. 'The person that got off had a hood. Was it a man or a woman?'

'I don't know,' she said. 'I couldn't tell, had a hood on. They are just shadows, driver's recollection. I was day dreaming on the way home.'

Well, I asked for that, thought Ross. 'Okay then. What else did they have? You said jeans. What colour were the jeans?'

'Black,' she said, 'But they were flapping, flapped when they walked past. When they got off the bus, I think they were flapping, lots of flapping.'

'Flapping,' said Ross, 'you mean like flares?'

'No,' she said. 'They weren't flares. They weren't flares. But they would have been seen by Dougie,' she said. 'Dougie's not on that bus. Dougie didn't drive the bus. He got off it with me.'

'Okay,' said Ross, 'I think that's all we need.'

'Dougie had a blanket,' she said quietly. 'I saw Dougie's blanket.'

'Where were you exactly when it happened?' asked Ross. He could see the woman shift in the bed. 'I was . . . I was outside my house, then went up and saw Dougie, but that wasn't Dougie. Dougie was later. Dougie had a blanket.'

Ross thought what it must mean for the woman to see her colleague killed, probably burned, crushed, and then to see a blanket cover him later on. No wonder she just curled up.

'Thank you,' said Ross, 'I'm going to do my best to see that you get some help. For the meantime, just go to sleep. Okay?'

'The woman with the hood,' said the woman. 'Big shoulders, I mean big shoulders . . . and a big butt.'

Ross wondered where this was going. 'How do you mean a big butt?' he said.

'It was like thin legs and then her bum, big bum. Yes, like a padded bum.' Ross made a note in his book, trying his best as ever not to query anything, then got up to leave.

'Did you see Dougie? Is Dougie okay?'

'I haven't seen Dougie,' said Ross.

'But you're the police, you'll know if Dougie's all right. Tell me if Dougie's all right.' The woman started to reach up in the bed. Suddenly, she made a grab for Ross but he was too far away and she tumbled, landing on the floor. Ross heard the sound of a nurse racing over. Together, they lifted the woman back onto the bed, the nurse tutting at Ross's carelessness. Well, he hadn't trained for this, had he? He was a police officer, not a nurse.

'I think you better go,' said the nurse. 'Don't come back for a while. This one needs her rest.'

'Well, thank you,' said Ross. 'Thank you both. I think I've got what I need. There'll be officers outside. Just keep taking care of this one.'

'Why?' asked the nurse.

'She's a witness in a murder investigation where quite a lot of people died on a coach.'

'Well, I got that bit,' said the woman.

Well, you should get the next bit, thought Ross. 'If there's any retaliation, if she's seen anyone who's actually done this, she could be a target for them. But don't tell her that. I think she's got enough on her plate.' Ross made his way out of the hospital, picked up the car from the carpark, and drove back out to the mobile incident unit. As he parked his car, he saw Macleod getting out of his own car and walking over towards the unit. He was suddenly approached by a number of journalists, microphones at the ready.

'Have you found Sasha? Is she on board? Is she amongst the dead?'

Macleod shook his head. The Inspector was clearly tired but had enough of these shenanigans. Ross walked across.

'I'll take it, sir.' Macleod suddenly became wide-eyed but then nodded and walked off.

'Have you found Sasha?' asked the woman.

'Police investigations are still continuing at this time. We have no knowledge whether Sasha was on board or indeed where exactly she is. We only have a filed report that she is missing and we have nothing to suggest anything untoward has happened to her. So far, we are not taking her case as an incident of murder or any foul play. There are a lot of detectives seeking her out.'

The woman continued to shove the microphone towards Ross, but he put his hand up. 'No, that's it,' he said. 'Time for you lot to go.' With that, he looked over at some police officers and waved at them. 'Kindly escort these members of the press to a more remote location. I'm not sure the inspector's very impressed that they got here.' Ross saw the fear in the men's eyes as they quickly ushered the press out of the way.

Ross turned towards the mobile incident unit. On opening the door, he saw Macleod sitting, fighting fatigue with a cup of coffee in his hand. 'Thank you, Ross,' he said. 'I'm getting kind of sick of them.'

'I think we're all sick of them, sir. We're all sick of Sasha.'

'Yes, enough on our plate. So, what did you find?' asked Macleod.

'Well, sir, school kid got off. But otherwise, the only thing

I have is someone in a hoodie with big shoulders, a big bum and thin legs.'

'Oh, well,' said Macleod. 'They'll be easy to spot.'

Chapter 8

Macleod put the phone down, feeling like hurling it across the room. The DCI had been on, demanding progress, demanding that they find who had done this. Macleod updated him on what he did know, but apparently, the person in the hoodie was just not good enough. Macleod advised that a disaffected teenage bomber may be the line they should take, but his attempt at humour didn't wash with the DCI.

It was lunchtime when Ross and Jona walked in and told him that they'd finally been able to identify all the remains, mainly through DNA checks and through statements. Ross put down a long list in front of Macleod and watched as the Inspector started to scan it.

'Get Hope,' advised Macleod. 'She needs to see this as well, and if Clarissa is around, her too.'

'I'm not sure she is,' said Ross, 'She's still down at the coach company. I thought she had ferreted enough.'

'Are you questioning our new sergeant?' asked Macleod.

'Well, she's been down there for a while,' said Ross. 'I mean, Kirsten would have been back by now. I had to do all this stuff on my own.'

'And you better get used to it,' said Macleod. 'Clarissa has not got that skill, but she's a ferret and she'll dig things out; don't you forget it. And she's also your superior, technically.'

Ross felt thoroughly rebutted, but he turned and smiled at Jona, who seemed to roll her eyes over to Macleod.

'I think we're all a little edgy,' said Jona. 'Probably best we just chill out.' There came a grump from Macleod. Ross disappeared out the door and two minutes later returned, with Hope McGrath, her red ponytail swinging as she bounced in through the door. Macleod looked up at his sergeant wondering how on earth she looked so alive. His shoulders sagged, his feet ached, and his knees were beginning to get pains, but Hope looked radiant and ready to take on the world.

'Ready when you are,' said Hope and found a copy of the names being thrust towards her. She sat down beside Macleod and they both looked carefully over the list.

'We got their names, but do we know who they all are?' asked Macleod.

'Mostly just normal people, there's a selection here going on holiday and we've confirmed that. I would say that probably fifty percent were headed for the airport either for business or for holiday, and the other half were there to pick somebody up, get a hire car, things like that.'

'So, nobody untoward?'

'Well, it depends what you mean by untoward,' said Ross. 'There's a guy there at the top of the list—he's known for handling dangerous chemicals. No criminal record, but when I talked to his friends they didn't seem surprised that he was involved in something like this.'

'Seriously?' asked Macleod. 'Or is that just idle chit-chat?'

'Nothing to back it up sir, but there are some other things

here. The good news is, Sasha is not here; we do not have a dead pop star.'

Macleod looked up to the ceiling and sighed. 'Thank goodness for that,' he said. 'We can do without the theatrics.'

'Anyone connected with the coach company?' asked Hope.

'No,' said Ross. 'No one except, of course, for our witness and Dougie Douglas, but as he was driving the coach, I doubt it was him. That's a spectacular backfire if it did.'

'Anybody else of note?' asked Macleod.

'We've got a professor on board from the university, mildly well known in his field.'

'Which was?' asked Macleod.

'Bio-molecular physics,' said Ross without hesitating. That's what Macleod liked about Ross. He knew his detail; anytime he quizzed him on it, it was straight back with an answer.

'Okay, Ross,' said Macleod. 'Anyone else?'

'We do have an Eamon McGinty, and he's got a criminal connection.'

'Now you're interesting me,' said Macleod.

'Yes, what is it?' asked Hope.

'In for GBH, at least twice. Number of other incidents involving him which couldn't be proved. Number of times, people backed out of making statements. He's reasonably well known to uniform, sir. He's never handled a police officer though; it's always been Joe Public he's hit.'

'You think he's a player of some sort?' asked Macleod.

'I don't know, but I tell you what. He certainly does have some lead-ins, or he could be involved in drug gangs; that's what the rumour on the street is. As I said, nothing ever confirmed. I'll start doing a bit more digging around him, sir, if you like.'

'Yes, you do that,' said Hope before Macleod could say anything.

'Better than that,' said Macleod, 'I'm going to go and break the bad news. I assume he has a wife.'

Ross looked down at his notes. 'A wife and kids, living out on one of the nice estates actually, the North end of Inverness.'

'Do you want me to come with you, sir?' asked Hope.

'No, I want you to go and find out the other side of this guy—get on the street, ruffle a few feathers, find out who on earth he actually was. I'll gauge the missus, you gauge the community, and we'll meet back and talk about it. Well, that certainly makes things more interesting, if we've got a potential drug dealer on board.'

'In what way?'

'Something Clarissa has said to me, we talked about the coach and the attacks on it, they had some low-level eggings, some scrapings, and broken wing mirrors, but she said this was more like a war. Why do you plant a bomb? You plant a bomb to make a statement. If you don't make a statement out in public, you've made the statement already,' said Macleod. 'What if this guy was the target?'

'You mean like a gang war?' asked Hope.

'Rumours of drugs,' said Macleod. 'It's a possibility; it's not a given, but we need to find out more about him because the rest of these characters you've passed on don't seem to fit any sort of bill. Don't understand why anybody would want to blow them up, and if you're blowing up truly innocents, well, then, there's usually some reason behind it. Some sort of banner to fly, a flag to be unfurled, and nobody's done that. I don't think this is terrorism. This is something else.'

'I'll get on it then,' said Hope. She stood to leave the room

69

but Macleod called her back. 'Just hang on a minute, Sergeant. Ross, you get back onto CCTV and details of all these people, make sure everyone's got a visit. Tick off the boxes because I don't want to announce numbers of dead, et cetera, until we know for sure that the next of kin have been informed. Will you cover that for me, please?'

Ross sighed but nodded. 'Of course, Inspector.'

'I assume you're continuing, Jona, hunting down more information?'

'The only other thing I have is that Semtex; the strain of it definitely comes from Irish dissidents.'

'I assume you're going to try and contact the Northern Ireland Police Force, see if they can furnish any more information,' said Macleod, 'although, who knows what that's going to bring. I think our best line at the moment is finding out about this potential criminal. See if he's at the centre of what's going on. It might be a punt in the dark, but it's the only direction I've got to punt at the moment. Let's get on with it.'

Just as he finished speaking, Clarissa burst in through the door. She saw an expectant room, awaiting the substance of her dramatic entry.

'Sorry, just tired. Didn't mean to startle.'

'Coffee on the side, I suggest you get some into you, Sergeant, because we've still got more work to do.'

'Do you know, when I was working on the arts' side, it was much more civilized, Seoras, much more civilized. You should be giving these people a break.' Macleod's face turned red.

'I'll thank you not to give them ideas,' he said. 'It's hard enough without the idea of a respite given to them.'

'We can all do with forty winks,' said Hope. 'Maybe we should rotate.'

'No. Maybe you should get off down to the town and find me some detail about our potential gang member.'

'Gang member? You got a lead then?' asked Clarissa. 'That is good because the coach company is a dead duck. I have gone through every single record; I have spoken to everyone. There's nothing going on down there, except some low-level hassle for some thugs. I swear the place is squeaky clean. From what I gather, anyone could have stuck a suitcase underneath that coach. I've just sat and talked to a number of employees, most bursting into floods of tears. What did I get from it? Dougie Douglas was a really nice guy. I get the image of a guy crushed up against the steering wheel and everyone telling me he was really nice. No way did he deserve that. Better at least we had somebody that deserved it up there.'

'We don't tend to speculate that much in our cases,' said Macleod. 'I appreciate you're a bit tired, but let's keep it to a strict level of what's needed to be talked about.'

Clarissa looked over at Macleod and gave a gentle nod. 'I hear you. I hear you. I'm just beat.' With that, she slammed a cup on the counter and poured herself a coffee before flopping down in the seat at the table.

'Maybe you're right, take an hour. Clarissa, get some sleep. After that, I think Ross might need a hand.'

'What about you?' asked Clarissa.

'I'm off to tell someone that her husband's dead,' said Macleod. 'Always the fun part of the job. Day or night.' The team watched Macleod stride out of the room.

Hope gave a little chuckle. 'He doesn't change, does he?'

'Is he right with this though?' asked Clarissa. 'I mean, nobody seemed to challenge him with his theories there.'

'There are no other theories,' said Ross. 'He's right on that.

71

It might be a wild goose chase with this guy, but at the end of the day, a wild goose chase is all we've got, so we'll do that. We'll come out the other side and see what's what. You must have had this in the art world, chasing down leads that come to nothing.'

'Of course, I have,' said Clarissa, reaching back behind her head, pushing her hair out with her fingers. 'I had plenty of dull leads, but this needs an answer. You saw all those bodies out there.'

'Easy,' said Hope. 'It's not the first time I've seen multiple bodies. Though it must be the most I've seen. It's horrific, but it can't drive your thought process. It can't force you to look for an answer when there isn't one.'

Clarissa nodded. 'I knew all that,' she said. 'It's just—'

'It's just how can you let something like that go unresolved?' said Ross. 'You can't, and we won't.'

'Anyway, I've got my orders,' said Hope. 'I'll see you back here soon.' She walked off, closing the door behind her.

'That girl has got some swagger.'

'I wouldn't really notice,' Ross said. Then Clarissa laughed. 'Of course not, love, course you wouldn't. Sorry. That's ridiculous isn't it, getting this giddy?'

'You haven't slept,' said Ross, 'so put the coffee away, go into your car, and crash out.'

'Go to my car,' said Clarissa, 'I only get an hour's sleep and the best I get is my car?'

'Well, you can drive home if you want,' said Ross, 'but do that and you'll be late back here, and you'll probably only get a five-minute nap. Got to learn to sleep where you can. If you're really lucky, we get to be somewhere off the mainland and then you get a hotel.'

Jona got up from beside Ross, shaking her head. 'I'll leave you two to the minutiae of good investigation then,' she said before walking out.

'Do you think he's right though?' asked Clarissa.

'He was quoting you earlier on,' said Ross.

'Seoras? About what?'

'Something about a war. You said something about a war coming. The coach bombing was like a war.'

'I did, yes. It is like a war zone, isn't it?'

'No, no. You've got him on some other trail. His head's thinking, he's looking for something big coming up, I can tell. He was worried there. Your comments, he didn't let them go. He's trying to focus us back in; that means he's worried.'

'Worried? Are you serious? It's a bit late to worry with all that out there.'

'No. He always tells you, you can't see the first one. You don't know what's happening. It's the ones after that. He thinks something else is coming.'

Ross stood up, walked to the door, and gave Clarissa a wave before he left. She sat back in her seat, looking at the coffee in front of her.

'Another one?' she said. 'I can't take another one.'

Chapter 9

Macleod glanced round at the estate where the home of Eamon McGinty was located and found an element of disgust in him that criminal sorts were occupying homes like these. The estate was brand new, and Eamon McGinty's home was one of the largest houses on it. Located at the rear, looking out onto the vast fields, Macleod noted that there were two cars out on the drive: one, a large BMW, and the second, a sporty run-around, possibly a Porsche. The lawn was meticulous, as if there was a gardener on hand to cut away any stray weed or piece of hedge that dared to peer out from its regulated place. At the back of the house, Macleod could see a swing and a large fort, not hand-built but made with real wood and stained eloquently.

'They say crime doesn't pay,' tutted Macleod at the police constable driving the car for him.

'It does make you wonder, sir, doesn't it?'

'Makes you wonder what?' asked Macleod.

Clearly, the constable hadn't realized that Macleod was annoyed at this and was not making some cheap joke. There was a moment's hesitation from the young man, but he recovered brilliantly.

'How they get away with it, Inspector.'

'They get away with it because we don't catch them. Pull up in front. If you'll wait in the car, I'll handle this.'

Macleod stepped out of the car. The front door opened as he approached it, revealing a substantial gentleman whose frame filled the doorway. His hands were clasped together, and he had a serious look on his face.

Macleod looked up, almost sneered at him, and asked, 'Would the wife of Eamon McGinty be at home?'

'Who wants to know?'

'Detective Inspector Macleod wants to know. I'm afraid I need to pass on some information to her.' The man stared at him before stepping to one side and letting him in. Macleod entered a luxurious hallway and noted the small chandelier above his head. He was directed towards the front lounge of the house, and on entering, he saw a woman sitting on a chair, tears streaming down her face. Behind her was a large china hutch with a large amount of crystal in the far corner. A modern TV, more than three times bigger than it needed to be by Macleod's estimation, faced a large sofa and around the room were photographs of the woman who was now weeping, along with a man. Kids also adorned the pictures, and it looked like the family home of someone with quite a bit of money.

'Mrs. McGinty, my name's Detective Inspector Macleod.' He took out his warrant card and badge, and a man stepped from beside the woman to inspect his credentials.

'And you might be?' asked Macleod.

'A friend of Mr. McGinty's,' said the man. This one was smaller than the man at the door, with a bald head and a taut chin, but he certainly looked like he could handle himself.

Macleod nodded. 'Sorry, I didn't catch your name.'

'Alan,' said the man.

Macleod thought about challenging him further but let it go. At the end of the day, he was here to see Mrs. McGinty, not the fellow gang members of Eamon. Macleod made his way over to the woman, who was crying on her soft armchair, and squatted in front of her. 'Mrs. McGinty, I'm sorry, but I feel I'm going to tell you something you probably already know. Your husband, Eamon McGinty was on board the coach that exploded on the way to the airport yesterday. My sincere condolences.'

The woman looked up, tears streaming down her eyes, 'Thank you, Inspector. I just heard. His friends here have just told me.'

'Okay,' said Macleod. 'Which one let you know?' he asked, and the woman pointed to the bald-headed man.

'That was good of Alan to do that,' said Macleod, wondering how the man knew or rather knowing that a leak had been made, one that he was going to chase through and hammer the culprit for. 'As I said, my sincere condolences, but I do need to ask you some questions, just about what your husband was doing and a few other things. Is there anywhere we could talk in private?'

'I'm not sure that the lady needs to be on her own at this time. The comfort of friends is always better,' said Alan.

'The comfort of friends is always good and kind,' said Macleod. 'That sort of friendship is always hard to find.' The bald-headed man stared back, but Macleod held his fix. He was aware what was going on, but he wasn't going to be outdone.

'You could do with a cup of tea,' Macleod said to the woman, who looked at him quite shocked. 'I could make it for you if you want, or maybe one of these kind people would do it for you.'

'They don't make it right,' said the woman suddenly. 'It's maybe best if I go through and make it. I could make you one too, Inspector. Why don't you follow me?'

Alan stepped across, almost instantly. 'It's all right, Erin. We can get it for you.'

'No, it's best if I do it. Best to do normal things, don't you think?' Erin McGinty suddenly stood up out of the chair, and Macleod saw that she was a thin woman with long hair to her shoulders. They'd obviously caught her unaware with the news, for she was in a sports top with lycra bottoms on, highly inappropriate for a widow. But then again, you never got to dress for the news, did you?

'No,' insisted Alan. 'I'll do it for you.'

At this, Macleod turned to the man. 'If Mrs. McGinty has asked to do something, I think it's best, at this time, that we respect her wishes, in the name of being good friends, don't you think?' And there it was. Macleod put the challenge on the line. As he did so, he looked around the room, staring at two other men. They were more like doormen, standing with their hands together, shoulders broad, almost waiting instruction.

'The Inspector's right,' said Erin. 'I need to go and do these things. Can you go and check on the kids at the back?'

'Have you told them yet?' asked Macleod.

'No, it's literally been twenty minutes. I don't think I can face them yet.'

'Best if you do it when you're ready,' said Macleod. 'Alan will look after them, won't you, Alan?' he said. The bald-headed man blinked, as if he wasn't quite sure what to do.

'Please, Alan, go see them, make sure they're all right. It's what Eamon would have wanted of you.' Alan made his way out of the room. Erin followed him, taking Macleod into the kitchen area.

It was a modern kitchen, and Macleod reckoned that Jane, his partner, would have climbed over you to get it. The large American fridge in the corner had a gleaming exterior with a digital display on the front. *Who needed a digital display on a fridge?* All it did was keep things cold.

In the garden beyond, Macleod watched the kids playing with a small push car until Alan approached and said something. The look of suspicion in the children's eyes said it all, and Macleod struggled not to laugh at the man's struggles to ask them a meaningful question and get an answer. Although he could not hear the question or the replies, Macleod could see the sharp retort of the children.

Macleod watched the woman make her way to the kettle, lift up the top, fill it up, place it down, and flick the switch. Macleod moved closer as he watched her put two hands on the sink and fight back tears. She said nothing for a whole minute. Macleod waited for the appropriate time to speak. As the kettle started to thunder, she turned to look at it.

'I'll talk in a whisper,' she said. 'Only when the kettle is boiling. I can't say anything with them here; do you understand?'

Macleod nodded. 'Was your husband going anywhere in particular?'

'My husband was always away with his work. I didn't know if he was coming back, or where he was going or when he would arrive. He just strolled in the door. I was here to be a good wife for him, to be his to use, something he could come home to. Trust me, Inspector, I'm not sad he's gone. Part of me wants to go up and shake the hand of the person that did it. But it's them out there I feel for. Those boys worshiped him. He may not have treated me well, but he looked after them.'

'I see. It wasn't easy being his wife?'

'No,' she said. 'Sure, he'd come home with presents and that, but it was always the same. Something to wear in the bedroom, something to wear when he was out to show me off.' Macleod looked at the woman. He could see how that would work. Maybe her best years were past her, but he still thought she could turn a few heads. The pity welled up in him for someone who was a trophy wife, not there to be loved, just there for the amusement of the man who kept her. 'They came in and told me,' Erin continued. 'I started to cry, but really there's not a lot to cry for. I haven't had much of a life. He controlled where I went, so it's good riddance, Inspector. Somebody's done me a favour.'

The kettle clicked and Erin began to pour it, but Macleod shook his head, reached forward, poured half the contents down the sink, and filled the kettle up again. After pressing the button, he waited for a good thirty seconds before the kettle began to bubble again.

'I understand why you're glad he's gone, but I need to know where he was going and did he have any trouble?'

'There's always trouble,' said Erin, 'always somebody he had to sort out. Understand me, my husband was a right bastard. Evil with it, too. I know. I suffered the physical side from him, but so did the people he was with. All of them in there, they would have been scared of him. I've seen many of these guys before. I've seen him hit several of them. There's the odd one or two that aren't around anymore.'

'You saying he finished them? Shot them?'

'I'm saying I haven't seen them. I didn't get to see that side of it. He was never daft enough to commit something like that in front of me, make me a witness to things, make the boys a witness. Instead, he would do it in the quiet, but certain people never came back, or they'd turn up all of a sudden with bruises. Accidentally fell over. I've had to do that a few times myself. He liked a bit of the rough stuff, and not mutually, Inspector. We all have our fun and games, but not like this.'

Macleod nodded and the kettle clicked again. 'I may need to talk to you another time,' said Macleod, 'when I find other things out, if that's okay with you.'

'If you can get me on my own. It won't be easy for a while. They'll be worried about me talking now he's gone. Worried I could say things, things I might know.'

'Do you know anything?' asked Macleod.

The woman shook her head. 'Eamon wasn't stupid. He kept me out of everything. Yeah, I knew that type of thing he did, but I knew no specifics. There's no court I can stand up in and grass on him. He didn't trust me for that. Thank God, he liked me enough not to put me in that position.'

'Definitely like, not love,' said Macleod. 'I'm sorry. I would say I'm sorry for your loss, but that seems a bit shallow. I'm sorry for what you had to take up to now and I'm sorry for your boys.'

'Thank you, Inspector. You'd better drink some tea.' The pair made their way back into the living room, where Alan shortly returned, standing at the side of the room, listening intently. Macleod asked some banal questions. Did Erin know where the man was going? How long had he been away from the house? It seemed that Eamon McGinty had been gone only that morning. Together they had dropped the boys at a nursery before McGinty had dropped her home again. He had then packed his bags. She assumed that he was going to the airport.

'He could be away for a couple of days at a time,' she said. 'But it wasn't always the case.' Macleod did not overstay his welcome, realizing there was nothing to be gained from talking in this cauldron. He made his way out of the house, back to the car, and the rather green constable within it.

'Did that go well, sir?'

'Things don't go well and they don't go safe,' said the Inspector. 'Things just go and you take from them.'

'And what did you take from that?' asked the constable.

'That the woman in there can't speak. Eamon McGinty was certainly part of some serious criminal activity. Also, that Mrs. McGinty has no alibi.'

'You think she did it?'

'No. There's nothing to indicate she did. There's nothing to indicate that she wasn't just here. She said he dropped her here and then he disappeared away. All I'm saying is she has no alibi.'

This is war. That's what Clarissa had said. He wondered how Hope would get on, talking to Eamon McGinty's boss. If they were quick, maybe they could stop a reprisal, but they'd have to know who had done it. More than that, they'd have to prove it. And in proving it, they would then be open to the whims of McGinty's gang. Would a police arrest and jail sentence be enough for the person that did this or not? And then, of course, there was the idea that McGinty was just an innocent passenger and there was something quite different that had gone on with the coach. *As ever, more questions than answers*, thought Macleod.

Chapter 10

Hope had to trawl through a large number of criminal records to find Eamon McGinty's contacts. Making her way down to Inverness, she found a rather disreputable bookmaker's and watched it for a while. Jerry Flanagan was the person she was looking for. He had long black hair, a man of forty-five who tried to look like he was twenty-five, wearing a baseball cap backwards, an oversized hoodie, and jeans that hung off his backside. Often, he was stoned according to the reports, but on other occasions, he could be seen at the bookmaker's trying to make enough money to get stoned again.

But the good thing about Jerry was he knew a lot of people. He knew who went with whom, who ran with whom, and who not to cross. Jerry was a survivor. Not a particularly adept one, because he'd had his kickings in his time, but for the things he got involved in, the fact he was still alive meant he knew who not to cheese off and who he could grass on.

Hope watched him enter the bookmaker's that afternoon. After telling her constable to remain in the car, she made her way in after him. Most bookmakers these days are rather neat inside, she thought. Gone are those days of cesspits, smoke in the air, swearing and cursing, and the scrunched-up bits of paper being handed back and forward. Now there are screens showing all the races, a clean counter with electronics and neat betting slips being passed back and forward. You can even pay by card, and yet this particular establishment still had the word seedy written all over it. When Hope walked in, every eye turned to her.

'Look at the arse on that,' said a voice out loud. Hope flicked her head to the right, saw the overweight man who had said it and walked over towards him. He stood glaring at her, almost daring her to do something. She reached inside her leather jacket, took out a warrant card, and slapped it in his face.

'You're lucky you get the warning. The next person gets hauled out of here. Gentlemen, there's a lady present and if you don't treat her like a lady, she won't treat you like gentlemen.'

There was a general murmur and then a man behind her gave a large wolf whistle and announced, 'Yeah, but he's right about the arse.' Hope turned, walked directly over to the man and grabbed his nose between her forefingers.

'I'm not allowed to break your bones, but then again, I could leave and come back in without my badge. How would that suit you?' she asked, twisting his nose hard, so much so that the man fell off his seat onto the floor. The others laughed at him until Hope raised her hand and turned and stared at them. 'Next time I come back in without the badge.' Then there was silence.

'You,' said Hope, pointing over to the corner where Jerry Flannery was trying to hide. 'I'd like a word.'

Flannery was shaking his head and Hope wondered if he was smacked up. She leaned over closer as he cowered in the

83

corner.

'Eamon McGinty,' she whispered in his ear. 'Who's his boss?' Jerry squirmed, trying to fit himself into the corner like some sort of frightened mouse. Hope leaned forward, grabbed his jacket and started searching inside. She pulled out a white packet.

'Tell me now,' she said, 'or you're down the station.'

'That'll break my parole,' he said.

'Eamon McGinty's boss, who?'

'It's Sammy Devine, but you didn't get that from me.'

'No, and you didn't get this back from me.' Hope took the packet, opened it and poured it inside the man's jacket. She shook it up a bit and several bits fell on the floor. 'Get your life cleaned up,' said Hope and then turned around, striding across the room and out of the door. Once she reached the street, she thought back to what Macleod had said to her once about keeping an eye on Clarissa Urquhart because the woman was an operator. Hope wondered how Clarissa would have *operated* in there.

Sitting back in the car, Hope asked the PC to drive downtown because the name of Sammy Devine was well known. He owned a couple of clubs in the city, but beyond that the force had been trying to gather evidence of his other dealings. Drugs, extortion, illegal gambling dens—Devine was into most things. There was even a prostitution ring, although they didn't believe the women were trafficked. Rather he was more of the main pimp, not that it made it any better.

Hope made her way to Devine's main club and again left her constable companion outside. On the doors of the club was a rather underdressed woman and there was certainly no doubt about what the sort of entertainment she would see inside, but things had not got going yet. Across the street from her, Hope saw a man shuffling past in a sudden rush when she glanced at him. Maybe he had been eyeing up the leggy woman in lingerie who was advertised on the doors of the establishment, or had he been casting looks at her?

Hope shook her head and then stepped up to the door. She found places like this difficult. Any exploitation was wrong, that was a given, but places where people simply enjoyed the more physical sights and sounds of entertainers were not something she had an issue with. Macleod would be raging at the scene, but Hope was only angry about the women who were exploited by people without integrity. That being said, she would not be here by choice.

There was a closed sign advising they would open up later that evening. Hope thundered her fist against the door, so much so that the door was flung open, and a rather ugly man shouted out, 'What the hell do you want?'

'I'd like to see Mr. Devine,' said Hope in a very calm voice.

'Mr. Devine doesn't want to see you,' said the man and went to slam the door shut.

Hope put her foot in it. 'Yes, he does. I've come from Macleod and we're not taking kindly to the idea that a coach just gets blown to smithereens. I want to talk to Mr. Devine about this. After all, McGinty was on board.'

The man's face dropped and he looked a little panicked. 'You can wait here,' he said. 'I'll go and see if Mr. Devine would like to see you.'

Hope forced the door open. 'I'm sorry,' she said. 'Mr. Devine is seeing me,' and she strode past the man into the club.

Hope was never a frequenter of these places and certainly Macleod hadn't been either. In their time they'd occasionally had to pop into a gentleman's club but rarely was there any activity going on. As Hope entered the main room, she saw a man sitting with a shot glass in front of him, watching two women on the stage. They were taking up angles and positions that Hope had never encountered in all of her relationships and she saw the delight of the man gawking at the women. Music thundered out across the room, and it was only when Hope was halfway across that the man caught sight of her and raised up his hands, instantly cancelling the music.

'You two, nice work, but get out. Looks like I need to talk to a real lady.'

'Mr. Devine, my name is—'

'Your name is Hope McGrath. You're Macleod's sergeant. Just because our paths don't cross doesn't mean I don't know my coppers and you're here because you've realised that Eamon McGinty was on that coach going to the airport. Am I right?'

'You are,' said Hope, hoping her face didn't show the unsettlement that was going on inside at her being recognized.

'Forgive the performance going on. If you'd let my man come and tell me you were here I would have dispatched the ladies before letting you into the room.'

'That would have been kind, but it doesn't really take away what you do with them, does it? I'm not here to be entertained,' said Hope. 'I'm here because—'

'You're here because Macleod thinks this could kick something off,' said Devine. 'But what makes you think we know anything about it? Why do you think it was for our man?'

'We have plenty of thoughts about who it could have been for,' said Hope.

'And yet you're here to see me.'

'Routine enquiries.'

'But yet there's no one with you. You're not here for routine enquiry,' said Devine, 'So let's not kid me.'

'Okay,' said Hope, nodding. 'I'm here because Macleod is worried that this bomb was set for your man.'

'And does he know that for a fact? Where did the bomb come from?' asked Devine.

'Have you much experience yourself?' asked Hope.

'I don't deal in that sort of thing. I deal in lovely women for my men to look at. You can accuse me of being a devotee to the female body but you can't accuse me of being a man who deals in bombs.'

'Has anyone upset you recently? I mean in a big way, or have you upset anyone else? If this kicks off, it won't be pretty.'

'If what kicks off?' said Devine. 'I haven't said I'm doing anything, and who do you suspect would do it? If I'm this figure that you think I am, who's going to challenge me? Why would they kill Eamon McGinty? He was nothing to me. Small fry.'

'Oh, you won't miss him then, and you won't be bothered.'

'You could say that. Certainly nothing to get out of bed over.'

Hope stared at Devine, trying to read him, but the face was immaculate, just a smiling glare at her. Behind him, she saw a couple of girls suddenly enter the room and then they turned to go.

'No, no, ladies. In and onto the stage.' Hope wondered why they suddenly looked embarrassed simply because she was there. The total lack of clothing disgusted her but she turned away, realizing that she recognized one of the girls. It had been maybe two weeks ago, and she'd been walking through the holding cells when she saw the woman being placed inside for drug dealing. Maybe she'd been given a warning. Hope thought she saw a chance to talk to someone who might know a little bit more.

Vacating the club, she sent the constable on to the station and waited outside. There was nowhere to sit indoors and have a good view of the club, so instead she walked round and round waiting for the correct moment until she saw the doors open and the girl she had spotted before, coming out. She had a large raincoat on now, but she strode along in high heels. Maybe she'd dressed quickly to get out of there. But whatever had happened, she was certainly fast on the move. Hope watched her jump aboard a bus and only just about managed to get on herself. The bus had an upper deck to which the woman climbed the steps. Then Hope followed her up top and along to the rear of the bus where she sat down beside her.

'Plenty of other space, love,' said the woman to her.

'There is indeed, but I think I'd rather sit with you. Though you have a lot more clothes on this time.'

The woman looked at her strangely. 'If you're coming in the club for that sort of thing, I don't do it outside, okay? There's no extras, no freebies going on.'

'No, but how does he pay you? If I have a look through that jacket pocket now would I find something?' Hope saw the woman tense. 'It's not good when you get hauled in, is it,' she said, 'because next time they might throw the book at you in a proper way. I don't know about you, but I couldn't do some of those things on stage unless I'd sniffed something up my nose or drunk a hell of a lot.' The woman looked out the window.

'In case you hadn't noticed my name is Detective Sergeant Hope McGrath and I need some information.'

'I don't talk about that place outside,' said the woman.

'Well then, we can talk about it down at the station after I do a stop and search on you right now and find the bit of powder that you don't want me to. You've really got to learn to keep a better face.'

The woman seemed to shake, mulling over her choices. But then she turned to Hope with an ugly sneer and said, 'Okay, what you want? But you don't tell anybody about it.'

'I only want stuff that anybody could know,' said Hope. 'You ever heard of Eamon McGinty?'

'Yeah, I heard of him.'

'One of Devine's men, isn't he?' said Hope.

'He wasn't one of Devine's men; he was Devine's rising star. He came into that club and shook most of the men around it up. From what I could gather, most of them were afraid of him. With good cause, too.'

'Were you afraid of him?' asked Hope.

'All of us were afraid of him, and not like we are of Sammy Devine. Sammy's a right nasty one if you cross him. See, if you don't, he's fine. He treats you okay. Sammy buys you clothes, nice ones. Yeah, sometimes, some funny ones. Likes you dressed up for him, but, you know, nice stuff too for walking about outside. He gets you gear as well. Keeps you in it. You play right by him, he's okay. You obviously don't drop things. I mean, this now, you don't tell him about this. If you do, I'd deny it anyway.'

'I won't tell him anything but tell me more about Eamon McGinty. You don't have to worry about him. He's dead.'

'They said that to me today. He was on that coach, wasn't he?'

'Do you know why he was on that coach?' asked Hope.

'No, I don't. I don't know why they go anywhere. But I'll tell you this, there's a lot of happy men in there today.'

'Why?' asked Hope.

'He wasn't liked. Right bastard. Not just to us but to them as well. I mean, if you got McGinty and he set his eyes on you, you panicked. He wasn't a nice man with it. And to the guys in there, if they were out of line and they challenged him—in fact, at times as much as look at him, he'd beat them to a pulp. But Devine liked that, his enforcer, and that meant that McGinty was moving up. You could see that. Some of the guys when we were entertaining would curse McGinty. You heard things about how he was moving. So yeah, I think most people are glad he's gone.'

The woman suddenly stood up. 'It's my stop,' she shouted back. 'Don't get off.'

Hope let her go, mulling over what was being said. Maybe this was an inside job. Maybe it was one of Devine's people, or maybe it was a rival firm that McGinty had just been a little bit too harsh on. Either way, the suspect list was growing.

Chapter 11

Ellie was tucked up in bed. This routine, in fact, was a boon to Ian, for now he could take his dog out for a walk. The collie was chomping at the bit, having been stuck in all evening while Ian had prepared tea, taken his wife up to the bathroom, bathed her, and got her to settle down for the night. It wasn't Ellie's fault, for the car accident had left her in such a poor state that the road to recovery was going to be long. She had to be helped everywhere, and she hated it as well. But now having done all his chores, including making sure his wife was comfortable, Ian was finally getting to stretch his legs with his favourite companion, aside from his wife.

The night air was cool for the time of year, and once he'd stepped outside, Ian wished he'd put on his full coat rather than the simple rain jacket he was wearing. But the rain jacket was fluorescent, a necessary precaution now that the night was fully dark. Sometimes they cut across paths and fields without lights, down the odd country road, and it was always best to be seen. James Boy, his collie, was also wearing a fluorescent jacket, and as Ian exited their small drive, the dog was already pulling at the extended lead, so much so that Ian let it off a little so the dog could move about freely for a while. The new type of dog leads was a boon. You could reel in the length of the lead whenever you wanted, but when there was time and space, the dog could run much freer yet still was under control. Not that James Boy needed much control. After the initial years of being what Ian could only describe as a 'little tyke', the dog had settled into life with them, still inquisitive, but obedient when called back.

'Where should we go tonight, James Boy?' asked Ian towards the dog. All he got was a simple cocked ear, and the dog headed off to sniff at something else. Ian let the lead pull in tighter, and soon the dog was walking beside him, tripping along at a brisk pace.

Ian and Ellie had lived on the estate for more than forty years. They'd seen changes, families come and go, and what had once been a relatively posh situation had turned into a lower-middle-class something of a place for those families that just struggled to even be comfortable. Ian and Ellie had no such problems. But they hadn't left, preferring to remain and do their bit for the community that had been their home for so long. With no children, they felt a bond to the area as if it was their baby.

Ian bent down to pick up some sweet wrappers that were on the ground. *Kids these days. Wouldn't have done that when I was young*, he thought. *Who am I kidding? Of course, we would. It's so easy to punish the young these days.* But there were things that annoyed him, of course there were. Everybody seemed so weak these days. Didn't seem to just want to get up and get on with it. Back in his day, you only got to boot up the bum for not getting out the door. Maybe it was for the best, he didn't know. After all, some people had ended up right messed up in his day.

Ian continued along, following a circuit he followed at least once every day. It took them out to the far end of the estate past some of what were now known as the dodgier houses. People had been placed there, people with problems, and a lot of the estate complained about it, asking why they couldn't go somewhere else. Ian thought that was unkind, but at the end of the day, everybody wanted a safe home for their people, didn't they? If you had a choice of living beside a convict or somebody who won the Mother Teresa prize for being thoroughly decent to people, who would you pick to neighbour with?

Ian chuckled to himself at this thought. Yes, he was out now with a chance to walk, think, put the world to right, with only the occasional whimper and whine because he wasn't walking quickly enough. As Ian continued along the street and passed a boarded-up house, he saw that several of the streetlamps were out. He wasn't the one to shirk away from something like that, just a little bit of darkness, and he continued with James Boy, stopping at the first streetlight, and looked up. Yes, it was smashed. That sort of thing he couldn't abide. *Why break something like this, something useful, something that's giving help?* He looked at the house before him, which was boarded up. *At least they've done it someplace where nobody lives*, he thought. He sighed and continued his walk.

A little bit of rain started to fall, and Ian pulled up the collar of his rain jacket and increased his pace. He cut across the road because the corner turned left, and rather than walk around the whole pavement in darkness, he thought he should move to the other side, where the light was. As he crossed the road, something caught his eye. He stopped and felt the jerk of his lead, as James Boy was continuing. A good dog, he understood that the road was not a safe place. As Ian peered into the darkness of the pavement they had come from, James Boy continued to pull.

'Easy. Easy. I know. Middle of the road. Let's go back over, this way. Come on, boy.' Ian made his way over. In the darkness, he thought he saw something attached to the streetlight. As he got closer, his heart began to pound. His eyesight, especially at long distance, wasn't great, and at the moment, the streetlight was somewhat of a blur, but it was in focus enough to confirm his belief he was looking at a couple of feet.

Ian began to jog over more quickly now. The shape started to take form, and he could see the jeans of what appeared to be a man's legs. Looking up, he saw them rise into a white shirt, but the shirt was stained somehow, although Ian was unsure what with. It wasn't like a ketchup stain. This covered almost fifty percent of the shirt.

Ian dropped the lead as he looked up and saw a face hanging off to one side. The man's arms were pinned back behind him, and Ian realized that he was hanging off the lamp post. Ian jumped onto the wall that ran behind and spotted that the man's arms were pinned together in some sort of a A-frame, the wrists bound, and then hung off a massive nail or was it a screw, that had been placed into the rear of the lamp post.

He reached up. The man's hands were still warm and he heard a gargle from in front, Ian put his hands past the man's wrist onto the nail that was holding him in place. It had been screwed in, a thread of some sort. They'd actually cut a screw thread and then put the screw in with it.

'Devine,' gargled the man. 'Bloody Devine.'

'I'll get an ambulance. Come on.' Ian heard the man choke and he began spitting out blood. Ian reached down to his pocket, grabbing his mobile phone. These small devices were a pain in the neck and he struggled, fumbling with it, trying to remember his code. He wished he'd just made it four digits of a single number. Maybe one, one, one, one or one, two, three, four, something that wasn't eluding him at this time. It should have been a simple thing to do, but he was panicking, failing to make his fingers work.

Ian could hear James Boy starting to bark and he watched the collie jump up at the lamppost, and then casually begin to sniff the man's feet. Ian managed to press the nine three times and he placed the phone to his ear.

'Which service do you require?'

'Ambulance. Police. Maybe fire service. There's a man stuck.'

'One moment.'

'Police emergency.'

'There's a man stuck up a lamppost, he's dying, I think he's dying. You might need an ambulance . . . no, you will need an ambulance. Maybe the fire service as well. Do you hear me?'

'Where are you, sir?' asked the voice on the other end of the line.

Ian detailed the street he was in, mumbling several times about what house number it was.

'And what is the condition of the man?'

'Bad,' said Ian. 'He's hanging from his hands on a lamppost. He's—' Ian leaned round to try to see the man's face. It was then he noted the gash around the bottom of his neck. 'I think his throat's been cut in some way. There's blood everywhere.' Ian's hand touched the shirt. It was wet, wringing, and his hand was now covered in blood. 'I'm going to try and get him down; I need to get him down.'

'We're dispatching units now, sir. Stay there.'

'Where the hell else am I going to go? The man's dying.'

'Devine,' whispered the man. It was almost a wheeze. Ian jumped down off the wall, reached up, and grabbed the man's legs. There was no way from the wall he could lift the man by his wrists and take him off the simple screw that was holding him, but maybe if he grabbed his legs and pushed up, the arms might free themselves.

James Boy leaned up against his legs while Ian wrapped himself around the legs of the man. He bent his knees, asking them to work again. They weren't what they used to be. After all, he had reached seventy years of age, but there was life in him yet. Before Ellie's accident, he was at all the clubs, golf, bowls, even a bit of tennis in the summer. He walked every day with the dog, so Ian was not unaccustomed to making an effort when he needed to. He drove up with his legs, felt the man began to move upwards. He tried to shake him, felt blood spitting down onto his back, peppering the rear of his head.

'Bloody hell, come on,' said Ian as he felt his legs would start to give way soon. With one last push, he shoved upwards again. Then Ian felt the weight of the man come off the screw and begin to force down on him. It shouldn't have been unexpected, but it was. Ian fell to the ground and the man came down with a hard smack into the ground. Ian was trapped under his legs and James Boy was standing at Ian's feet, sniffing, seeing if his master was all right.

'Get off, boy, I'm fine.' Ian was able to sit up, but his legs were trapped under the man. He went to push one away, but the man toppled over into him, leaning up against him.

'Dear God,' said Ian. 'Look at you, dear God.' Ian placed his hand over the man's throat close to where he'd been cut. He could hear the man rasping for breath.

'Devine,' he said in a hollow gasp, 'Devine.'

'God? You're talking about the divine?' said Ian. 'Yes, you'll see him soon, but not if I can help it. Come on. There's still time, son, come on.'

'Devine. Bastard. Devine is a bastard.'

'Don't take that attitude with God. I know it doesn't look good, son, but come on, keep going. Keep going.'

The man's head slumped again to the side and he seemed unable to lift it again. Ian continued to hold him, urging resistance until the lights of the police car arrived. The constable who jumped out of the car was able to lift off the man's legs and Ian rolled to one side. He lay there watching the officers attend to the man. They attempted CPR, but it was difficult until they cut the hands away from behind the lamppost, for the man had still been bound to it, even though he was leaning up against Ian. As Ian lay and watched, horrified to the core, James Boy came and sat beside him. Ian wrapped his arms around his dog. 'I know, boy, I know.'

Chapter 12

Macleod took a call in the middle of the night just as he was finally getting some sleep. His partner Jane had picked up the call and it must have been important, because she had learned by now to fend off anything trivial. Her mind was tired, thoroughly exhausted, so if this wasn't important, they would get both barrels from her.

He'd got up, had a shower, and then made his way towards the estate on the edge of Inverness where the body had been found. On the way, he picked up Hope but let the rest of his team sleep. They'd soon be told about this in the morning.

The street was now lit up in contrast to earlier, a number of configurations of powerful lamps positioned around where the body had been. There was a tent made around the lamppost with only the very top of the fixture appearing out, and Macleod could see the forensic van already on scene. As he approached, a constable acknowledged him.

'Inspector, we've cordoned off everywhere, not allowed anybody near it. Fortunately, it's the middle of the night so we haven't had many people come for a look. I'm not sure how many people know about this yet.'

'Good,' said Macleod. 'Let's keep it that way, although it's not easy with the noise of investigating, is it? Where's the man who found the body?'

'Ian Sterling. Sent him home to his wife. It's not far, just a couple of streets around. In fact, he wasn't that far from home, really. He was out walking with his dog, spotted the guy up on the lamppost, went to attend to him but he had difficulty. It seems that the man was hung up on the lamppost. Mr. Sterling had to lift him off. Sterling then fell underneath the victim. Fortunately, he'd made the call to us by then. When we arrived, we were able to lift him out of the way. We tried CPR, everything, but the man was dead.'

'Any idea who he is?'

'Yes, one of the boys recognized him. His name is Frank Egg, quite well-known amongst the drugs division. They said he's not at the bottom, rather more of a high-ranking member.'

'Did he say who he was in any organisation?'

'No,' said the man. 'I can give you a number to contact. We got them up because they thought it could be tied into the drugs.'

'Good lad,' said Macleod, 'I will need to speak to them. Who's the forensic lead on scene?'

'Jona Nakamura's out, sir. She said she had a bad feeling about this.'

'I'll see her directly then,' said Macleod. 'Hold the perimeter. I'll be back to talk to you later.'

The constable nodded and Macleod made his way over to the scenes of crime van. No one was inside, so he dressed in a coverall suit, accompanied by Hope, and they made their way inside the tent.

Macleod was used to murder scenes but he still stepped back when he saw what was in front of him. A man in jeans and a white shirt, albeit a shirt that was now heading more towards pink and red tones, was lying against the base of the lamppost, his arms bent backwards in a bizarre direction. Macleod could see the cut close to his neck.

Jona Nakamura looked across from the far side of the tent. 'Inspector, I'm afraid this may be the beginning of your worst fears.'

'How so?'

'This looks like punishment. The man's been beaten up badly and then he's been taken, hung deliberately on the back of the lamppost. He must have been in pain, but they cut him. I reckon that Mr. Sterling must have found him maybe ten minutes after it started, possibly less.'

'Not easy to hang someone up there, I'd have thought,' said Hope.

'No, you'd certainly need a couple of them. I think he's been struggling as well so there might have been a number. It was done in the dark, the streetlight wasn't working as a lot of them in this area haven't been. You'll notice a lot of the houses are boarded up too, Inspector. They found somewhere quiet. This wouldn't have been an easy job to do. Hang him off the back and then screw at the top, that's been put in beforehand. If you put a thread like that in, it would make a lot of noise in the dark. That's been there for a while.'

Macleod shook his head at the idea that this was pre-planned, that somebody at some point had thought if a punishment to be carried out, this is how to do it.

'How long do you think he was hung there for?'

'I would say ten minutes. He hasn't been able to call out

because they've cut into his windpipe. He could say things and indeed the witness said he did speak, but it would have been more of a gargle, forced effort, quite hard to say. He was also hanging with his arms behind him. His lungs were compressed down. This would hurt, sir, really hurt.'

Again, Macleod shook his head. 'Have you got anything more for me on it? I've been told it's Frank Egg. I'll get some details from drug squad about him, but anything else you can tell me?'

'Not really, Inspector. I haven't been here that long myself. I'll try and get DNA off him to see if anybody's left any tell-tale marks, but this was well-planned so I doubt it. They knew this guy was going to die and it was going to be painful; that's all they cared about, and then hanging him like that.'

'That's a public statement,' said Hope, 'isn't it? This is what Clarissa was talking about. This is war.'

'Let's hope not,' said Macleod. 'Let's really hope not.' He made his way back out of the tent, pulled down his hood, and sought out the constable who'd been there when he arrived. After finding out from him which officers had first attended the scene, he made his way towards them.

'What's your name, constable?' asked Macleod looking at a rather shaken individual.

'Constable Peter Davenport, sir.'

'It's just Inspector, if you want, you can call me, Seoras. Not a good one, was it?'

'No, Inspector, it wasn't.'

'Did the man say anything, indicate anything when you got here?'

'To be honest, he was already pulled down at the time we got here. We tried CPR, we had to cut the bonds from his arms.

101

He was lying in a rather crazy state. We tried but there wasn't much hope, throat been cut, blood everywhere.'

'Say anything?'

'The guy just kept talking about God.'

'God?' queried Macleod.

'Didn't realize these sorts of people were that close,' offered Hope.

'What did he say exactly?'

The constable pulled out his notebook and flipped it open. 'Divine, bastard divine. Something about God, the witness said. Talking about the divine all the time.'

Macleod nodded. 'Thank you, constable. Get yourself cleaned up and look after yourself on this one. That wasn't pleasant.'

'No, sir.' Macleod walked away a short distance. Hope followed.

'Devine, he's calling Devine. It is a gang murder.'

'Looks like it, Hope. I'm going to phone in for some details. Let's get an address, see if we can find out a bit more about this Frank Egg. We can send somebody else round to the witness, see if he said anything else. We'll place a call that way as well.'

Macleod picked up the phone and rang in looking for someone with the drugs division. He got his equivalent and he spent a couple of minutes on the phone and received information about Frank Egg's history. He was from a rival gang to Devine's and was known as an enforcer. He was up to his neck in plenty of nefarious goings-on. They tried unsuccessfully to pull them in in several drug busts, but the man was always clever enough to be out of the way at the time.

'He says he was a nasty piece of work,' said Macleod. 'I'm not that disappointed that he's out of the way but their Inspector realized the potential of this. This could kick off badly, Hope.'

'Indeed, sir. Did you get an address?'

'Yes,' said Macleod, handing over a slip of paper.

'Oh, very nice. These guys certainly have money, don't they?'

'It's probably his home pad. He probably has plenty of other places to hang out when things get rough, but let's go check it out.'

Hope drove west of their current position into a classy estate, but this time the home they came to was one of the smallest. It shared a building with three other flats. Macleod made his way to the front door of the ground floor flat and banged on it. There was no answer. Macleod glanced at his watch. It was 5:00 in the morning. Maybe he should have treated everything with a little bit more decorum, but after he saw no movement, he thundered his fist on the door again. The door beside the one he was banging on opened and a woman in her dressing gown stood looking at him. She was shortly followed by a man in boxer shorts.

Taking a look, they went to close the door quickly but Macleod called over. 'It's fine,' he said. 'Detective Inspector Macleod,' and he pulled out his warrant card and badge. 'This is Detective Sergeant Hope McGrath behind me.'

The door opened fully and the couple stood looking at them. 'We don't think Mr. Egg's in,' said the woman.

'Do you know where he is?' Macleod saw that pair look at each other, heads down.

'If you're worried about Mr. Egg bothering you, he won't. Mr. Egg is sadly deceased. I'm trying to account for his movements tonight.'

'Okay,' said the woman. 'All we know is that he went out earlier on tonight.'

'About what time?' asked Macleod.

'Eight o'clock.'

'Are you sure about that?' The woman nodded. Macleod looked at the man. 'Was he with anyone?' The couple looked at each other again. 'Look, I don't need to know or broadcast who you are. I'm trying to work out what's happened to this guy.'

'There were a couple of people, men who came, knocked the door. Mr. Egg went with them. Well, I say went . . .'

The man behind the woman took over. 'It looked like he was hauled out of there,' he said. 'We didn't get a good look at who did it. They were just a couple of men, medium height, thickset. You don't ask about what Frank does. He wasn't the best of the neighbours, to be honest. Grumpy, told you nothing about what he was doing, asked you all the time what people were about. That's why we got a little bit worried when we opened the door and saw you, we thought it might be somebody high or drunk. We were going to chase you off in case Frank came back and did you in.'

'Did you get a lot of that?' asked Macleod.

'Well, I don't know for sure, but I've always thought Frank was involved in like, drugs and things,' said the man. 'So, I kept well out of any of his business, but he occasionally got a bit of a dropout turning up. He always gave them short shift, very rough with them.'

'I understand,' said Macleod. 'You didn't see any of the faces of the men that came?' The man shook his head.

'How long is . . . sorry, was Mr. Egg here?' asked Hope.

'We've only been in six months,' said the woman. 'Not long married. We didn't realize he lived here. To be honest, we wouldn't have bought the house. It's probably a good thing that he's gone for us, though it's not a nice thing to say, is it?'

'By the way he's been carrying on, I think that's a fair thing to say,' said Hope. 'Probably going to have less hassle now.'

'Did they take him in a car?' asked Macleod.

'More of a minibus,' said the man. 'It was blue. No idea about a registration plate, before you ask.'

'Make?' asked Hope.

The man shook his head. 'No, I don't deal with car makes.'

Macleod looked at the man and the woman in front of him. She was shaking and he saw the man's hands grip her shoulders firmly, but the man was also agitated. Macleod could see sweat forming on the side of his neck.

'Look, I know where you live, and I understand that you're not going to be able to give me a lot of information. I don't blame you, given the type of person that Mr. Egg was. If I need more, I'll be back for it but if you can't identify the people or maybe give me a description and not give me much more than on the van, there's not a lot else for me to say except you'd do well to keep out of this. If anybody else comes to the house, don't ask, stay clear. Saying that, I'm probably going to be here with a search warrant to go through the place in the next few days. It's a lot of the trouble, so keep well away. Thank you for your time, Mister—'

'Tom. Tom and Jane.'

Macleod thought that was a lie and he looked and smiled. 'I know where you live. I know your house. Your names won't be that difficult, but I get you're scared, so please, go back inside and keep well out of it. Thank you for your time.' Macleod watched the door close as he stepped away from the house back to the car.

'I doubt there's anyone in there, sir,' said Hope. 'Sounds like they came, took him away, did him in. There doesn't seem to be a lot of point going in there. Best to let somebody like Jona get in.'

'That's exactly what I was thinking. Let her get in first, see if she can pick anything up. If they had to haul him out, she might get some DNA. No, I think we're done here. Now we know it's Frank Egg, I think I need to go in and talk to my drugs counterpart. Get a full briefing on what's going on between this lot.'

As he reached the car, Macleod assessed the estate he was in. There was money, not as much as some others but it was here. But here was also a type of reticence, or was it fear, that he had never known growing up. In his day, everyone knew their neighbours and you would lend a hand if they needed it. More than that, everyone had seemed to know everyone else's business as well. Back on Lewis that was seen as a universally good thing, but Macleod had his doubts. Not that the kind of neighbourhood relationships he had just seen were any better.

Macleod's phone rang. He picked it up, seeing it was the station.

'Macleod.'

'Sorry to bother you, Inspector, especially as you're already out, but there's been another murder. A woman found on the beach.'

'Whereabouts?' asked Macleod.

'Down under the bridge, sir. I've already got a hold of your other sergeant. I believe Sergeant Urquhart's already on route.'

'That's understood. Get hold of her, tell her we're on our way over as well, and you had best contact Jona Nakamura. I think she's going to be required here as well.'

Macleod closed the call and looked at Hope, who was

standing with a quizzical look on her face. 'Another body,' said Macleod.

'Where?'

'Kessock Bridge, at the bottom.'

'Linked?'

'Possible,' said Macleod. 'This close together, seems likely. Let's go find out.'

Chapter 13

Clarissa Urquhart jumped into her sports car and tore away from her flat located in the centre of Inverness. The streets were quiet at this time. She drove fast, feeling her hair blowing behind her as she headed off with the convertible top down on her vehicle. This was partly to keep her awake as she drove, for she was feeling the pace of this investigation. She had maybe managed four or five hours of sleep before the rude call that awoke her. She hadn't even had time for a shower before jumping into the vehicle.

She arrived at the Kessock Bridge from the south but knew the body was on the far side, so she drove over it, made a left turn about half a mile away from it and drove down through Kessock, getting as close to the underside of the bridge as she could. Thankfully, she had put on some hiking boots; no stylish shoes as she clumped along. With her tartan shawl wrapped around her, she made a bizarre figure as she approached the constable on scene.

'I'm sorry, ma'am, you can't go any closer. There's been an incident down here. I'm going to have to ask you to go the other way.'

'You should really be asking me why on earth a woman of my

age is parading along here at this time of the morning wrapped up in a shawl and boots. Surely you might have wondered if I have something to do with the incident.'

The constable looked at her. 'I'm afraid, ma'am, that I don't engage in that sort of a conversation. I've asked you to turn and go back.'

Clarissa shook her head, reached inside her shawl and took out a warrant card and badge. 'Detective Sergeant Urquhart. You called me. Kindly take me to where the body is.' The constable almost bowed in apology. Clarissa followed him across a number of rocks to where he pointed down to the edge of the shore. Clarissa saw the blonde hair of a naked woman, her back turned with her legs stretching out and her feet just dipped in the water.

'Any chance of a tide coming in and grabbing that body?' asked Clarissa.

'No, ma'am, it's on its way out,' said the constable.

'Okay, so that gives us, what, maybe twelve hours? Have we called for the forensic team?'

'Yes, Jona Nakamura is on her way.'

'Understood. Has anyone spoken to the Detective Inspector?'

'Which one?' asked the constable.

'You're quite new, aren't you?' said Clarissa.

'Only been working in Inverness for three weeks, Sergeant.'

'Detective Inspector Macleod will want to be informed about this. Make sure he's been called.' Clarissa dismissed the man with a wave of her hand, and slowly made her approach towards the body. She wouldn't touch it, just take a look to see if anything was lying around her.

The woman had an all-over tan. That surprised Clarissa as

she had to do that deliberately. If somebody had a bikini line, they were just one of those people who maybe caught the sun, liked to sit out in it, but generally, those who had an all-over tan worked at their figure or took it out of a bottle. From the colour of the skin in front of her, this was no attempt from a bottle.

Clarissa scrambled ungracefully, her shawl hanging loose around her as she got down close to the face of the woman. The hair obscured her slightly. Taking out a small pencil, Clarissa moved the hair back so she could see the woman's face. There was hardly a blemish on her, although she was heavily made up. Lipstick, makeup that Clarissa thought would probably break off if you took a chisel to it, and eyelashes that defied belief.

After a quick search of the area, Clarissa didn't find anything else, so made her way back to the edge of the cordon. As she did so, Jona Nakamura arrived, but this time, in her car, rather than the forensic van.

'Miss Nakamura, good to see you.'

'Jona. Just call me Jona. Where is she, Clarissa?'

'Just down to the edge. I've done a quick skate around and I haven't touched the body. Merely had a look at her face. Have you got any suits in the bag?'

Jona opened her boot, took out two coveralls, throwing one to Clarissa. Once dressed, the pair made their way down to the body. Jona took out her mobile, snapping photographs of the woman's position. She then bent down and gently lifted up her arm and ran her hands underneath the body.

'There's nothing in the rocks underneath I can find,' said Jona. As she lifted the body up, Clarissa caught a full view of the woman's figure.

'If I had been built like that, I wouldn't be doing this job.'

'I'll just put her back down,' said Jona, gently placing the woman back in the position she had previously been in. She then made her way down to the woman's rear, and after a few minutes delicately moving her legs and examining her lower regions, Jona stood up and stepped away from the body.

'She's definitely been abused,' said Jona. 'Need to do a better investigation to tell us exactly what's happened, but she's been sexually abused, and at some point, somebody stuck an arm around her and choked the life out of her.'

'A bit of a strange one,' said Clarissa. 'Why would you do that and dump the body here? I mean they've missed the tide if they were hoping she would disappear. How long do you reckon she's been dead?' asked Clarissa.

'She's actually reasonably fresh. I would say she's probably been dead for four hours maximum. Something like that.'

'Can you get a photograph of her face?' asked Clarissa.

'Yes.'

'Send it to me on the phone. Just something I want to check up on.' Jona nodded, and as Clarissa took off her suit, she heard the beep on her phone, a message arriving. She then took the attached photograph and sent it to the drugs division at the station. Picking up the phone, she was surprised to hear that many of them were actually in the office.

'What's the crisis,' asked Clarissa, 'since you're all up?'

'Haven't you heard? Your boss has been out most of the night.'

'No,' said Clarissa, 'I've called him to come here but he hasn't arrived yet.'

'He's been out. Frank Egg's been murdered.'

'And he is?' asked Clarissa.

'He's one of Devine's rivals. Your boss is worried a gang war might be setting off. What did you want from us?'

'Just sent you an image into your email. Have a look at the face; tell me if you recognize it.'

Clarissa heard the man type away on his computer. There were a few seconds of silence as he looked up the picture, but then the man let out an almighty swear.

'What's the matter?' asked Clarissa.

'That's Devine's bird. That's his bit on the side. Not his missus, the one he really likes. This is the one, this is her.'

'When you say that, what do you mean exactly?'

'Devine's got family,' said the man. 'Couple of kids and that, but then he's got the woman he actually wants, and this is her—Maggie. Maggie Brown. She's been with him for a year, probably year and a half. Lives in a separate flat. All hell's going to kick off now.'

'When did Frank Egg die?' asked Clarissa.

'According to your Inspector, he got jumped right about seven o'clock last night. Was dead towards midnight or beyond.'

'But would they know he was dead?' asked Clarissa.

'They didn't need to know he was dead, but they knew he was jumped. Word gets around in these places. If you can't get a hold of them, you go round; the neighbours tell you what's happened. Heck, this is big.'

'It is indeed,' said Clarissa. 'The boss has just arrived as well. I better go speak to him about it.'

She closed down the call and made a way over to the vehicle bearing Hope and Macleod. As Macleod got out of the vehicle, he stared at Clarissa.

'What's the worried face for?' he asked. 'Are you okay?'

'I'm fine,' she said. 'You're not going to be. Dead female down by the water; it's Maggie Brown.' Macleod looked at her, bemused. 'Maggie Brown is Devine's bit on the side.'

Macleod's face fell. 'How long has she been dead?'

'Jona's done an initial examination—reckons around four hours. I hear you were out to Frank Egg. This looks like a tit for tat.'

'Yes indeed,' said Macleod. 'I'm calling a conference; we need to deal with this. We need to get on top of it.' Macleod turned his back and put his phone to his ear. Hope strolled forward with Clarissa.

'You'd better take me down to see the body then,' said Hope.

'By all means,' said Clarissa, 'I think she's one of those girls. Well, she is one of those girls; that's what they said back at the station, but she's got a hell of a figure. You can see why he chose her.'

'Good to get some uniform down to canvass the area, but there's not really a lot here, is there?'

'No,' said Clarissa, 'but you could also do the stop and ask on top of the bridge. Start asking people if they saw anything down below. It's a long shot, but you can see the bottom of the bridge from certain angles.'

Hope looked up. The Kessock Bridge was above them, an impressive structure that spanned the Moray Firth, just beyond where the River Ness poured into it. Away to the right, Hope could see the lifeboat at the edge of a large marina and if you continued up that way, you'd eventually head towards the Caledonian Canal.

'Any indication she was dropped from a height or off the bridge?' asked Hope.

'No,' said Clarissa. 'She's in pretty good nick. Jona reckons she was strangled; however, she also thinks she's been sexually abused.'

'Well, yes, that would make sense, wouldn't it? Poor girl. Best grab my suit then,' said Hope. 'We'll make our way down.' Together, they walked over to where the main forensic van had now arrived. Jona was standing beside it, giving instructions out to her people.

'Are you okay if we take a quick look?' asked Hope. Jona nodded, handing a coverall suit over to her. Hope began to dress but Clarissa's attention was taken by a figure she saw beyond the cordon that had been established. It was a man wearing a police jacket, but she noted that he had jeans on underneath.

'Have we got anybody out here from any other department? Anybody else running this job?'

'Not that I'm aware of,' said Jona. With that, Clarissa turned and ran.

'You, what are you doing?' The man ahead of her turned and gave a quick look, his brown hair flopping out behind him. He made his way quickly down the rocks. Clarissa continued.

'I said, you, what are you doing? Stop.'

The man stumbled on down across the loose rocks, and then stood looking at the body. As Clarissa got closer, she watched him bend down, pick the woman's head up by the hair, and look straight into her face. Clarissa was only a few yards behind him now, and he suddenly hurdled the body and took off along the shoreline.

'Hope,' shouted Clarissa, 'got a runner.' The man continued to run hard along the shore. Clarissa found herself jumping from rock to rock. Her foot slipped, she felt a sharp pain, but she continued on, focusing on the man ahead. He doubled back heading up the slope and Clarissa fought hard working her way up. You didn't get this sort of action in the art world. It was all about being a character to someone else.

The man cut back trying to break through the cordon. He threw a punch, putting one of the constables on his backside, but it slowed him. Clarissa was now right behind him, and flung herself forward, wrapping her arms just below his knees, forcing his legs together. The man toppled over and fell hard. She jumped on his back, pulling the arms behind him before applying her cuffs. Sweat was pouring off her, and she breathed deeply.

'You just stay there, sunshine. You just stay there while I get a little bit of breath back.' Clarissa shook her hair out behind here then looked up at the face of Macleod peering down.

'I see you still have it. Well done, Sergeant. Very well done.' He addressed the man. 'Who are you, sunshine?'

The man refused to answer, keeping his face to the ground, so Clarissa hauled him to his feet so he was forced to look at Macleod.

'The Inspector asked you a question. Who are you?' The man kept his lips shut tight.

'He's one of Devine's,' said Macleod. 'I reckon they heard. Sometimes this police force has got too many leakers. Do you know that, sergeant? Somebody out there is passing on when things happen. That's why he's here because they don't know who it is. Somebody is missing, aren't they? Were you looking for Maggie? Did Devine send you?' The man remained silent.

'Get him in the car,' said Macleod. 'Take him down the station. Good work, Sergeant. Very good work.'

Clarissa marched the man to the car brought by Hope and Macleod and placed him into the rear. There was no way she could take him in in her little sports car. She instructed a constable to stay with the car and watch the man, before she made her way back to Macleod. She was puffing heavily and felt the morning cold as a slight wind cut across her face.

'You're expecting me to get your coffee for that one, are you?' asked Macleod.

Clarissa looked at him. 'I'd like to see you do that. I think I'm in better shape than you are, Seoras.'

'You may well be right.' Macleod saw the raised eyebrow. 'Anyway, it appears they've taken his trophy and killed her.'

'Looks that way. Damn pity—gorgeous looking girl,' said Clarissa.

'Too good-looking to be involved with that sort of thing. Why do they do it?' said Macleod. Clarissa shook her head. 'No, really, why? A girl like that, she could have any husband she wanted, surely.'

'We all make mistakes, Seoras.'

'Well, we can't afford to make too many here. Looks like you're a prophet.'

'A prophet?' asked Clarissa.

'You said the bomb looked like war. Well, it looks like it's coming.'

Chapter 14

Macleod stood outside the interview room awaiting his sergeant. Part of him was annoyed she was running late, but in fairness, she'd just been in a rugby tackle with the man. Now that she was back at the station, she needed to freshen up. It was better Clarissa was ready for this interview than appear dishevelled and not with it. The murder investigation team was a different place from the other departments and Macleod had years of experience.

He always felt that he could put his game face on in an instant. With his newest recruit, albeit she had significant time within the force, he was prepared to cut a little slack. Clarissa appeared, having changed, and was now wearing a smart pair of black trousers, a red blouse, and a black jacket over the top. It was quite a change from what she normally wore. It struck Macleod that this could possibly be her courtroom appearance.

'You okay?' asked Macleod. 'Ready for this?'

'You don't have to babysit me, Seoras. You're right I'm ready for this. What sort of a guy goes and picks up the head of a young dead woman like that, just to try and clock who she is?'

Macleod had ascertained the man's name from various records. Thomas Anderson was a lowlife within Devine's group. Now Macleod intended to squeeze him as much as possible to find out what was really going on between the rival gangs.

Clarissa opened the door and ushered her boss through first, keen to make sure that the man inside knew who was calling the shots. Macleod didn't wait for Clarissa, instead sitting down at the single table opposite the man on the other side. After he let Clarissa do the formalities while switching on the tape, Macleod sat back allowing her to take the opening lines.

'Thomas Anderson, I found myself called out to the body of a woman underneath the Kessock Bridge and while there, you snuck up close, taking a look at her. Do you have a fetish for naked dead women?' asked Clarissa. 'Or, is there some other way you can explain your presence?'

The man looked sheepish. Macleod enjoyed the tactic that Clarissa was using. Depending on who was on the other side of the table, if he had any sort of decency inside him regarding women, to put a woman on the opposite side, challenging that decency usually unsettled him.

'I was just there to make sure who it was.'

'To make sure who it was?' asked Clarissa. 'Why did you think it was anyone that you would know? Why would you look at a police cordon, walk into it, and examine the dead woman? You could've come to us. Asked us. Maybe given us an idea of who it was you were searching for because clearly then you were searching for someone. People don't pass by under the Kessock Bridge like that.'

The man's eyes started to flit around the room. Clarissa continued, 'So, tell me, why were you there? What had you out at that time of the morning? Just checking up on your handiwork?'

The man reared. Macleod almost laughed because anyone

with an ounce of sense would query why anyone would check up on their handiwork after having killed someone.

'I didn't touch her. She's a friend.'

'What sort of friend? Clearly, somebody was doing friendly things with her. We can check you know. Check who's been doing things. Things left behind. Semen. Body hair. If you were at her, if you abused her before she died, even if it wasn't you who killed her, we'll find you, you know that. Especially now you've been arrested for interfering with a crime scene. We have your DNA. We can check through.'

'But I didn't touch her. I'm on her side.'

'What do you mean, "on her side?"' asked Clarissa. 'What side does she sit on?'

The man choked, realising he'd made a mistake. 'I was just checking for someone. She's not my girl.'

'Whose girl is she?'

'I don't know.'

'You don't know. So, you know she's on some side, but you've no idea whose girl she is. You were checking up for this person you don't know.'

Macleod leaned forward. 'We know you work for Devine. We know that's Devine's girl. All hell is about to break loose, and you need to start talking, sunshine, or I am throwing you under the bus.'

Macleod sat back, turned briefly to Clarissa, and gave a small nod.

'As my Inspector says, you're going under the bus with this one. I suspect your DNA is going to be on her. I reckon you know her a lot better than some people think.'

'Maybe, but I didn't do that sort of thing with her.'

'What sort of thing?' asked Clarissa.

'You know, she's not my girl. I'm not making love to her. I'm not taking her to bed. She's not my plaything.'

'So, whose plaything, is she?' asked Clarissa. The man looked across at Macleod and back to Clarissa. 'Okay,' he said. 'She's Devine's girl. He has a wife, but it won't be any news to her if you tell her. The wife and the kids, that's for show. This is his playtime. If we're honest, this is the one he actually loves.'

Macleod leaned forward. 'So, why were you checking up on her? Why were you going looking? What's happened?' Again, Macleod sat back.

'She went missing.'

'From where and when?' asked Clarissa.

'She just went missing, okay? She's meant to be in her flat. Devine calls. She's not there. Well, he's a suspicious thing. Thinks she might be cheating on him because he always thinks that. She never has. She's never put one foot out of line. I think she actually did like him. He says to me, "Go check," because I run her places. If she's meeting him, I bring her. I make sure the Mrs isn't about, or wherever else he's going to, and I get her there. So, he says to me, "Go find out," because he trusts me with her.'

'What did you find?'

'I went to her flat in town. It's one of the posh ones towards the centre of town, up the top floor of this suite of flats. Knocked the door. Nothing. Well, Devine has given me a key because if she isn't doing things, isn't behaving, I'm allowed to go in, check nothing's wrong.

'So, you're what, a keeper? A guard?'

'Just a friendly person watching out for her.'

'Well, you didn't watch that well, did you?' said Macleod. 'I can't imagine Devine's going to be impressed with you.'

The Inspector knew he'd hit the nail on the head as he watched the man begin to shake.

'You don't have to go out again,' said Clarissa. 'We can put you away somewhere, work a bit with you, helps us with our inquiries. You'll get charged with interfering with a crime scene and nothing else. We can get that commuted down, do something with that and you disappear, because as you say, he's not going to be happy with you.'

'Were you meant to be watching her? asked Macleod, slightly suspicious.

'Yes. He's been edgy,' said Thomas Anderson, 'very edgy since that bomb went off.'

'Eamon was one of his boys, wasn't he?' asked Clarissa.

'Wasn't just one of his boys, but on the way up. Look, you can get me on the move, can't you?'

'I can get this tampering with a crime scene put to one side,' said Macleod, 'then you're on your own. You understand that? On your own, but that's only if I'm happy that you've told me everything and I want to let you leave. At the moment, you're telling me stuff that I know.' Macleod sat back again.

'The thing was with McGinty, he was on the move, working his way up, not liked by a lot within our group. Put a few guys noses out of joint and handy with his fists if you got in the way. McGinty pummelled you. Devine liked that though because McGinty was very loyal to him, but the man was fierce.'

'You must have been used to fierce people though?' said Clarissa. 'Must be used to people who are happy to go the extra distance, use a bit of GBH and that.'

'Well, yes,' said Thomas. 'You have to be able to handle yourself, but he was beyond that. He was talking to this guy one day, had a proper fallout. The guy hadn't done what he should have done, but McGinty turns around, has it ready to go with him. Pummels him and the guy is lying there, blood coming out of his nose. Suddenly McGinty's son is outside the door and his Missus is out asking where he is because McGinty had them in another room while he was sorting this guy out.

'He calls the son in and I kid you not, he lifts him up by the throat, holding him up against the wall lecturing all of us, telling us that as much as he loves his little tyke, he says if he ever betrayed him, he would finish him. The kid is up there practically wetting himself. In fact, he did. The kid pissed his pants. It was wrong. What kind of a person does that? The wife standing there, not able to say a word. Something else. Well the guys didn't like him after that, even ones that were trying to get along with him, but I'll tell you something, we didn't cross him.

'Then this bomb goes off, taking out McGinty, the boss's star man. Well, the boss wasn't happy, was he?'

'So, what did he do?'

'Shook some people down, got the word out, trying to find out what was going on. He got a tip—someone called it in. He never said who it was, but they reckoned Frank Egg knew who the bomber was.'

'What happened to Egg?' asked Clarissa, acting as if she didn't know.

'I heard they roughed him up, but they didn't get anything out of him. Solid to the last, he was. I don't know where he is though. I didn't get told about that.'

Macleod leaned forward. 'You don't think it could have been one of your guys not happy with such a cruel man stepping ahead of them. You have to have worked for him for a long time, wouldn't you? You wouldn't feel safe. Did you feel safe,

Thomas?'

The man shook his head. 'No, but none of us were daft enough to do that. It's a bomb. You don't turn and blow someone up with a bomb when they're inside the organization. No. All those other people gone too. Now this sounds more like Egg's gang. Say what you like about Devine, but don't bring the public into it. He only messes about with those who mess him about. The other lot couldn't care less. You could be somebody just standing there, you see something happen, or be next to somebody who owes him something, next thing your legs are gone, or he's whacked you. Bomb is more their style. Devine's right; that other lot would blow everybody up.'

Macleod leaned forward again this time his arms on the table, hands interlocked, and stared at Anderson. 'As it's started, is this going to continue?'

'You think,' said Anderson. 'They've just killed his bird? She was special to him. He'll be livid. He will hunt down every single one of them and when he starts that, you know what they'll do. There you go. I've told you what I know. Now, let me go, because I'm getting out of here.'

'Where?' asked Clarissa. 'Just exactly where are you going?'

'Norway, Sweden. I don't know. Bolivia. Anywhere away from here. This is all going to kick off. As soon as I saw her face there, I knew it was all going to kick off. Yes, I saw you coming for me, but I wasn't just running from you, I was running. I was going to get in my car, and I was just going to drive south and when I hit that channel, I was going to go on a ferry and keep going, because this is going to explode, but can you blame me? Bombs? A bomb taking people out, disposing of them.

'I mean, Frank Egg, I didn't like him. I hated the bastard, but we didn't do that, you know? Not like that. Devine said he was going to make a public example of him. From what I heard, they hung him from a lamppost. What's that got us? Maggie Brown, dead. From what you said, I take it they gave her a seeing to beforehand. He'll think that's been them all. He'll think she's been taken amongst them all and well, you know.'

Macleod felt a shiver from Clarissa, but she held her face, not giving away any emotion despite what had been done to a fellow woman.

'What about the bomb?' asked Macleod. 'Where do you get that sort of a bomb?'

'I don't know,' said Thomas. 'I have no idea. I don't do bombs. Look, he never sent me to kill anyone or rough people up. Don't get me wrong, Inspector. In my time, I've seen them go and break people's legs, but I have never been to see an actual murder. I've heard them do some. I know it's happened, but they were extreme cases. People you couldn't really trust. People that would drop you in a minute. People that gave them no way out. You keep it as clean as you can. That way you don't bring attention because what's important? The money. The money is what's important to these guys. This is no mafia. We're not protecting any community or that. It's all about the money, and it's not good business when you just dispatch people and bring a lot of heat on you. Always better to threaten.'

'I heard,' said Clarissa, 'that your boss was threatening the coach company.'

'That'd be right,' said Thomas, 'but again that was low level. We didn't attack any of the drivers. It's public transport, isn't it? Suddenly the government gets involved—much more heat. People can travel safely on a bus. Don't touch the drivers. No. Just a quiet bit of damage here and there. Looking for a low level of money coming in.'

'It wasn't Devine planting a bomb on them? Trying to turn attention away from him when they realized it's gone too hot.'

'Devine's no mug,' said Thomas. 'The coach company low-level steady income, that's what he's looking for. Bit of extortion here and there. Help fund the business. Nothing more and nothing less. He isn't into bombs. He isn't into mass murder. It's not him or at least it wasn't him. Now they've taken out his beloved. Oh, God knows what's going to happen.'

Macleod nodded to Clarissa, who ended the tape with the appropriate words and the pair left the interview room. Once outside, Clarissa turned to Macleod. 'What do you reckon then, boss?'

'I think it's time we get to the bottom of this because if neither of these sides planted this, we're going to have a gang war over nothing. If they did, we need to put an end to it quick.'

Chapter 15

Upon leaving the interview room, Macleod had gone straight to his desk and called the DCI. Half an hour later, he was sitting in a large conference room with heads of other departments and the DCI was opening the meeting. After a brief introduction, the DCI handed over to Macleod, who spent the next half hour detailing out the case and the fact he was ready for a gang war. Fielding various questions, he advised that all units should be on the highest of alerts and asked the drugs division to start putting out more feelers to find out what was happening on the street.

The Inverness drug scene was not known for its heavy-handedness, either by the police or by the dealers, but that could all change with the likelihood of guns being involved. Macleod asked that the standby unit be brought up to full readiness for armed response. When Macleod left the meeting an hour later, he returned to his desk, sitting behind it, and remained there for the next twenty minutes. When he hadn't moved, Clarissa Urquhart stood up from behind her own and made her way over to Macleod's office, knocking the door before entering.

'What's the next move, Seoras?'

'The next move is that we find who did this. Everyone else can cover off the war. Everyone else can try and see what's happening with that, contain it. We're a murder investigation team. We are not designed for that. What we need to do is what we are designed for. Solve this murder, the initial one, not the other two. Then, we start bringing people in. Show them what happened. Hopefully, it will calm down.'

'If it doesn't?' asked Clarissa.

'If it doesn't,' said Macleod standing up from behind the desk, 'then the other departments need to get on top of that and shut it down. But as of now, you need to be very careful. We're going up against people who will use guns, weapons. These are not basic murder suspects anymore.'

'How do we solve what's been going on then?' asked Clarissa. 'We've been going through everything.'

'I'm going to see Ross now,' said Macleod. 'We need that hooded figure. We need to know where that hooded figure went. I've got a problem at the moment. I've got Eamon McGinty who is not liked by his own side. He's on the way up. He's moving into the place and he is distressing people by doing it. But then we also have the other side. McGinty's an operator for Devine. Maybe the opposition wants him out of the way and if that's the case, we need to haul them in for it. We need to get everyone from all these murders together, highlight the cause to stop what's happening. We've got two lines we need to investigate: the hooded figure and where that Semtex came from.'

'Ross is where we go to next?' asked Clarissa.

'Yes, it is, but get a hold of Hope and bring her in, too. A number of eyes always helps.'

Five minutes later, Macleod joined Clarissa who had brought

along Hope. There were three people sitting in the video room where Ross was once again gazing at hours of tape accompanied by two constables.

'Tell me you got something for me, Ross,' said Macleod. 'I could really do with a breakthrough at the moment. Things are about to get very heated.'

'The hooded figure, sir. I've been trying to get more interviews down at the bus station. I can't get anyone who saw them put their luggage onboard. I also haven't got anyone who's able to say if it was a man or a woman. We're looking at a possible teen. Thin legs but a bit stockier here and there. They grow up a little bit misshapen at times, don't they?'

'You don't sound convinced, Ross,' said Macleod. 'You don't sound to me like you are sure of that person.'

'The trouble is with the interviews,' said Ross. 'It just gives such a wide range. Some people say it's a youth. When I ask "Did you see the face?" they say "No. It's behind the hood." The one person who would have seen the face is the driver, and he's not there. The camera onboard the coach is destroyed. Every other camera never picks up the hood except from the side or the back.'

'Deliberately?' asked Clarissa.

'Are we saying that this person knew what they were about then?' asked Hope. 'They deliberately wore a hood, kept themselves clear. Probably put their luggage on in a melee so that no one would see them actually put anything on.'

'Does the bus driver stand outside?' asked Macleod. 'Is he there watching people put luggage on?'

'He does several times,' said Ross, 'but if he was watching the hooded figure, they wait, and then move in when there's a lot of people. Also, I think at the time they place their luggage, the bus driver is distracted.'

'They're making sure that the bus driver doesn't realize they have a bag?'

'That's correct, sir,' said Ross. 'As I understand it, this person is very smart. I'd say they've done this before.'

'Professional hit?' asked Clarissa. 'Do you get that? Professional bombers?'

'You get hitmen of all sorts,' said Macleod. 'Could fit the motive as well. I mean, a hitman doesn't care who he kills at random as long as the client's happy with it.'

'Thomas Anderson said the other side would be. Not his own side but the other side. Their rivals would happily blow everyone to pieces.' Macleod sat down on the only spare chair in the room. 'How did they buy the ticket? They have to have a ticket to be on the bus. How did they buy it?'

'I've gone through all the transactions, both card and all the other inputs. What was left on the onboard machine was that the ticket bought for the stop where the hooded person got off was paid for with cash.'

'Blast,' said Macleod. 'There's got to be something else, some other way to trace. Have we checked where those hoodies are available?'

'Numerous stores,' said Ross. 'I can't track them down on the clothing. It's too wide, sir. Too wide. I've been at this for the best part of several days now. There's nothing else there. I've gone over and over and over. You need another line of attack. I'm sorry.'

Macleod shook his head, stepped forward, and put a hand on Ross' shoulder. 'I know. I know you've got it covered and I know you're all over it. I know you've been under a ton of stress because Kirsten would have been with you on this, picking a lot of it up, helping coordinate. You did a good job, Alan. Stay with it. You know I know. But go over it again, and again. Make sure there isn't something that jumps out or something in the background. Keep at it.'

Macleod walked out wondering if his pep talk was enough. Ross was such a conscientious worker. He'd barely left the station since this all started, the only time being when he'd gone to interview the off-duty driver. When they had first met, Macleod had found the man's sexuality hard to stomach. He had been brought up being cautioned that people like Ross would be cast into the fire. Macleod's faith had developed and while he still struggled with such a lifestyle, he tried his best to live at peace and only ever be positive towards those who did not share his own desires.

But Ross was more than just an officer with a different sexuality. Macleod had come to depend on him, even more now that Kirsten Stewart, his former DC, had left. And Ross had never failed him - Ross had even taken a bullet in front of Macleod. Sometimes you don't realise how good a person is when you meet them, he thought. Sometimes we have friends around us we never thought of.

Macleod made his way back to his office, sat behind his desk with a pad of paper and a pen in front of him. He wrote the word 'Semtex' with a question mark after it. Beneath it, he wrote down, 'Devine' and then 'McGinty'. Who could have killed McGinty? He drew an arrow from Devine, but he wasn't convinced. McGinty apparently hadn't done anything against Devine to warrant McGinty being blown up. Devine had also ordered Frank Egg's execution. Of course, he could have been covering up with that, making it out to be the other side but if so, it had spectacularly backfired on him as his woman had just been killed.

Jona was having a particularly difficult time. The bomb had been spectacular, of course, and forensic had been drafted in from other areas, but they had only been able to show one thing about the bomber: everything was done cold and clinically. Every report coming to Macleod had no other DNA, nothing to identify anybody else on the scene except his own officers.

Macleod stood up from behind his desk, made his way out into the main office, and poured himself a coffee. As he glanced up, he saw Clarissa looking at him, but she sheepishly darted her eyes away when she realized he was staring back.

'Hope,' said Macleod, glancing over at his sergeant, 'the office, please.' He turned with his cup, walking back into it.

Hope McGrath followed him, sitting down on the seat in front of the main desk, but Macleod continued to stand behind, looking out the window. What was universally recognized was one of the most disappointing views in Inverness.

'What's going on, Hope?' asked Macleod. 'Somebody wanted to start a gang war?'

'Who?' asked Hope. 'That doesn't make sense. Devine's doing quite well from what I can gather. When I talk on the street, he's their main man. The rivals aren't getting anywhere. Why does he want to kill them off? Why dispatch them? If he does, why do you blow your own man up to do that? I think if Devine wants to start a gang war, he'd have done it by simply going over and blowing somebody's head off,' said Hope. 'That's how you do it, isn't it? I mean, I know you've probably never started one yourself, sir, but that's what I would do. I wouldn't blow up somebody within my organization.'

'But somebody who's a rising star that strikes fear into everyone. Someone that they might fear more than you, so it's

131

a possibility,' said Macleod.

'Everything's always a possibility,' said Hope, 'but not in this case, no. This could be the other side, stepping up.'

'We'll need to go and see them, won't we? I'll need to go and talk to the drugs section, make a note who these rivals are, go and see the top man.'

'That might not be a wise move,' said Hope. 'I mean, what are we going to do? Just barge into wherever they are? If they are killers like this, why are they going to be bothered about blowing away a few coppers? This side's dangerous, Seoras. I don't think this is the wise move. You need to get them when they're not expecting. Get them where they're happy, relaxed, and you have something on them. Find out their haunt, the place they go to chill out, the one they know is safe, the one they think nobody's coming in to deal with them.'

'And then walk right in? Is that what you're suggesting?' said Macleod.

'Exactly, Seoras, but also, what are we going to do? Go inside and appeal to their better nature? If they planted this bomb, there is no better nature. You've got no evidence it was them. No evidence that actually, this was the start of a gang war, do you?'

'It had crossed my mind,' said Macleod. 'How many people on that bus? Forty-odd? And we're honed down on one person, one criminal connection, and we have followed it religiously since it's come up and gone for the jackpot. I have to keep reminding myself it may not be right. There may be something else here, or we may just have a complete nutter. Someone who just wants to see the damage.'

'Well, either way,' said Hope, 'we'll need to bring an end to this quick, so I say go talk to the drugs section. Find out where these people are, find out where they like to relax, go in, and see them.'

'I might just do that but you're coming with me,' said Macleod.

'Happy to,' said Hope, 'but I'd organize an awful lot of backup around this as well.'

'If they see us coming in with a lot of backup, they will be out of there before we have a chance to even get close to talk to them. This will be dangerous, Hope. That's why I'm taking you, someone that knows how to handle danger.'

Chapter 16

Macleod was waiting in his office for Clarissa's return so that they could head out to find Devine's rival gang boss. Having spoken to the drugs section, Macleod discovered the rival gang boss went by the name of Declan O'Malley, running a crew that has a distinctly Irish feel about them. Currently, he was under surveillance due to the situation that was occurring and was currently in a sports club on the edge of Aviemore. Macleod was still waiting for the sergeant to join him when he heard a knock at his office door. Jona Nakamura entered with a pleased smile on her face.

'Inspector, I might have something for you.'

'Well, let's hope so, Jona. We're kind of running on empty here.'

'The Semtex used in the explosion. I have a colleague working further south who found traces of it, the same type, same constitution. He believed it's heading up north. I thought I should bring it up to you straight away. I haven't got much more detail, but I'm sure if we coordinate, you might have more of an idea of where it's heading.'

Macleod placed a pad of paper and a pen on the desk in front of Jona. 'Give me the name of the contact and I'll get on it.' He watched Jona scribble down a number and a name, and as she was about to leave the office, he called out. 'Jona, if you can shout Hope to come in on the way out, it would be much appreciated.'

When Hope entered the office, Macleod smiled and saw her eyebrows flick up curiously.

'Where am I going?' she asked.

'Jona's managed to get a connection with the Semtex. It's one of the other departments further south. Get onto it, find out what's happening, chase it through, whatever you can pick up from it. We're running on empty here, Hope, so if there's any chance of a lead, follow it.'

'I thought you were going over to see the other boss today,' said Hope. 'You sure you don't want me with you?'

'No. This lead's too important. You're my senior officer. You follow it. I'll take Clarissa with me, much easier. Frankly, she's more likely to put the boot in than you.'

Hope looked downfallen. 'It's only a joke,' said Macleod, 'but seriously, you could learn how to develop a nasty side from her.'

'A bit old school—is that what you're saying, Seoras?'

'Yes, it is,' he said, 'and maybe she could learn a touch more class from you. You're thorough, Hope. That's why you're going, and you can handle yourself on your own. Clarissa's street-wise. If she gets into a fight, she's not built like you, but watch yourself. There's a gang war going on. Don't get caught in the crossfire.'

'Says he, going into the lion's den,' laughed Hope. 'Don't worry, I'll be in touch.' She spun round and Macleod watched her walk to the far side of the office, putting on another jacket.

Hope spent a little bit of time at her desk before departing and nearly bumped into Clarissa Urquhart who was coming in the main door.

The first time Clarissa had been with the murder investigation team, she was very brightly dressed, almost flamboyant, and Macleod noted that each time she came into the office since, the colours were being turned down a touch just a few shades, but enough to notice, certainly for a police officer of his experience. Just now, she'd entered in jeans, smart, black, albeit with a trendy pair of shoes underneath, yet with a short heel. On top, she wore a white chemise, but the pink scarf was still flung around her neck. Macleod kept an eye on her as she tied up her hair. Then he realized he'd been spotted.

Clarissa entered his office. 'Do I look presentable then? Suitable?'

'You don't have to look suitable to me. Haven't you heard? It's a new age.'

'The day you enter new age, Seoras, will be the day I follow you. I'm just toning it down a bit. I'm not all brash and colour.'

'Yes, you are and there's nothing wrong with it,' said Macleod. 'Stop trying to fit in. What do you think my view of you is? Be you, that's why you're here. I didn't fight for you to be here because you were a sergeant. I fought for you to be here because you're good. But watch yourself when we go out there. Hope just said we're going into the lion's den, and she's right, but don't buckle. Follow my lead. You don't have to stay silent, just keep with my tone. We're probably looking at the guy who murdered Devine's girlfriend.'

Clarissa nodded, turned on her heel, got to the door, and casually looked over her shoulder. 'Shall we go then? Or are you going to hit me with another pep talk?'

Before Macleod could say another word, she was away. There was something about the woman that touched at the insides of Macleod, something wonderfully abandoned. He saw shades of his own Jane in her and he had to check the warm glow he was feeling inside. *Time to get on, Seoras. Let's go*. A determined grin appeared again on the stodgy face.

'Ross, we're going to be out for a couple of hours. I'm on the mobile, keep me updated. Text only though, don't ring me. I'll ring you back if necessary.'

There was a wave from a desk in the far corner. Ross seemed to be consumed in paperwork. Macleod felt bad about this, but at the end of the day, that's what Ross was good at; it was his job.

Macleod insisted they take Clarissa's small green sports car. She put the hood down as the day, although cool, was sunny. Macleod wondered what people must have thought looking at the two of them driving along. Some old couple out burning around. Did they look wonderfully quaint, or did he spoil it? But the one thing about the car was that it shifted and soon they were at the sports club in Aviemore, sitting in the car park.

Macleod picked up his phone and contacted their man in the drugs division who told him that Declan O'Malley was still inside. Together, they walked in through the front door and past reception where a young girl asked Macleod if he was looking to swim. He ignored her and continued along to the restaurant where there was a viewing gallery into the pool. He could see a number of well-built men lounging around in swimming trunks, but none of them seemed to be enjoying themselves. Rather, they seemed to be keeping a distinct cordon around the sauna. Macleod pointed through the window.

'He's down there. He's in that sauna. Don't get caught up. We go straight down, straight in, face to face.'

Macleod tore off down into the men's changing rooms and heard the short heels of Clarissa Urquhart following him. As he turned into the changing room, several men were standing there with nothing on, drying themselves with towels and there were yells of complaint as Clarissa entered the room. Macleod marched out and skipped over the foot wash onto the side of the pool. A lifeguard, a young lad maybe nineteen, climbed down from a highchair. As he reached Macleod, he found a warrant badge and card shoved in his face.

'Back up on the chair, do your job,' said Macleod. He didn't wait for an answer, instead letting Clarissa encourage the young man back up onto his high seat.

As Macleod approached the sauna, a large man stepped across his path, but Macleod feinted to go to one side, then to the other, and walked past him. As he made his way further, two men stood side by side, offering no way around them. Macleod stopped and looked up at them. Behind him, he heard a splash as someone entered the water. A few seconds later, Clarissa Urquhart stepped in front of him.

'If you don't mind, lads, the Inspector needs to see your boss.'

'But the boss doesn't want to see him. I think he should retire.'

'I don't think you understand,' said Clarissa. 'My boss wants to see your boss. You need to stand aside. I will then stand aside and they can talk.'

Macleod, while anxious to get to Declan O'Malley, was enjoying himself, watching his newest officer handle the pair.

'I'm afraid that's not going to happen,' said the largest of the two men. He put his arm forward, looking to push Clarissa back. She moved to one side, slapped one half of a pair of cuffs on the man before reaching and grabbing the other man's wrist. Before they knew what was happening, she'd cuffed the two of them together.

'Step aside,' she said.

The two men now both tried to get her. As they moved forward, she stomped hard on the foot of one man, then the other, causing them to wince. She then pushed with all her might up into the rib cage of one of the men who stumbled, then tumbled into the swimming pool, taking the other man with him. Macleod wiped down some of the water that had splashed onto his trousers.

'Don't leave those cuffs in there,' said Macleod, 'I'm not sure what chlorine does to them.' Then he opened the door to the sauna before any other men from O'Malley's crew could reach him.

Inside the sauna were three men. One probably close to his seventies, with grey hair parted on one side, sitting with just a white towel on. From the photo fits given to him back at the station, Macleod knew this was O'Malley. The two either side of him were his protection. When they stood up, Macleod held up his hands.

'Don't. My name is Detective Inspector Macleod, and somebody put a bomb on a coach.'

The two men either side of O'Malley went to stand, but he raised his own hands. 'A delight to see you, Inspector. What can I be doing for you?'

Macleod noted that behind him, Clarissa was now standing in the doorway, and he saw the eyes of the two bodyguards watching her.

'The coach was blown up with Semtex, Irish manufacturer. Definite link,' said Macleod. 'Also took out Eamon McGinty, nasty man. Very nasty. He caused a thorn in a lot of people's sides. Rising star of Mr. Devine.'

Declan O'Malley showed absolutely no shock or surprise. He sat back nonchalantly, allowing the sweat rolling down the side of his face to drip onto his body.

'What do you take me for, Inspector? I don't do stuff like that. I don't blow people up. A lot of people on that coach. If I'm honest, Eamon McGinty, good riddance. Like you said, nasty boy. Kind of people Devine would use. He's got no class. You know that. They say the Irish are extra wild. You say we're reckless. I'm not that reckless. If I had a problem with McGinty, there's no way I'd have taken out a whole bus. Sounds more like a terrorist event.'

Macleod nodded. 'That's what we thought, but nobody's claimed.'

'No point being a terrorist and not telling people why you're doing it, and there's no way it was me either.'

'Why?' asked Macleod.

Declan O'Malley stood up, his towel barely hanging off his hips. 'Andy, Tommy, kindly step outside with the good lady at the door. I think the adults need to talk together.' Macleod turned around and looked at Clarissa, giving her a nod. When the sauna door closed behind him, Macleod sat down, aware that there was a condensation running onto his trousers. He reached up, unbuttoned his shirt, pulled his tie out slightly.

'If you want, I can get you a towel. It'd be much easier.'

'I'm not here for a social visit,' said Macleod. 'If you were responsible for this bomb, I am coming for you.'

'But something tells you I'm not, doesn't it?' said O'Malley.

'I've heard of you. I've seen the reports. You're a smart cookie. You'll get your person. You fear Macleod, that's what they said, fear you. Well, I don't fear you, Inspector, because I have nothing to fear. I did not touch that coach, and Semtex, I have no need of it.'

'What about your dealings with Devine? You're not denying you haven't had any.'

'Fisticuffs, bit of rough and tumble. That's it. It's never got to the point of killing anyone. A few guys might have had the odd broken arm, got a good seeing to, and that's it.'

'Does the name Maggie Brown mean anything to you?' asked Macleod.

'Of course,' said O'Malley. 'Lovely-looking woman. Sad though to keep her away like that in a flat.'

'Maggie Brown's dead. Frank Egg is dead. You can see, sitting here, why it makes sense to me. Maggie Brown had a visit from some of your people.'

'Of course, Inspector. It makes sense, doesn't it? Little bit of gang warfare, little bit of tit for tat. It doesn't do any good. Frank Egg is not one of my crew. Worked with me but not one of my crew. That was Devine. You can be sure of it, Macleod, but he's not come for me. He's not sure about the bombing either. He's looking at his own people. He's worried. He's worried he's got an internal problem. That's why it's Frank Egg. Frank Egg was taken out because he belongs to nobody but he's given me a message. Do you understand? He said, 'If it is you, I'm coming,' but he's got to sort house first.'

'So, what? You didn't go near Maggie Brown?'

'No,' said O'Malley. 'Maggie Brown has a long history with people like Mr. Devine and myself. Maggie used to be with me. I threw Maggie out when she started seeing Devine, but

I wouldn't kill her, a lovely lass but a daft one. Don't get me wrong, I'd love to have her back. Too much of a liability, but Devine liked that about her, a dolly bird on the side. But maybe she knew something. Maybe they're clearing house. You tell me, Inspector.'

Macleod stood up, walked to the door, but then turned back. He stared at O'Malley, then made his way forward again. 'You'd better be right because if this escalates, I'm coming for you all.'

'Inspector, understand, business is good. I have no need to establish more territory. Any tit for tat is bad for business.' Macleod nodded and walked out of the sauna to find Clarissa standing with four men around her. Two of them were dripping wet and still handcuffed together.

Macleod heard Declan O'Malley open the sauna door behind him.

'If you don't mind, Inspector, can we get the handcuffs off those two?'

Macleod nodded, 'Indeed. Maybe you need to teach them a few more manners. They thought they were going to handle a lady.' Macleod saw O'Malley stare at Clarissa who gave him a hard stare back.

'That's no lady,' said O'Malley; 'that's an outright tiger,' and he burst out laughing. When Clarissa took the key for her cuffs and undid them, O'Malley came forward still dressed in his towel and stood beside her. 'My apologies, ma'am. A little bit overprotective, some of my boys. You two, escort this delightful woman and her boss to the door.'

Clarissa was a conundrum to Macleod. She was a rank too high to be working under Hope and in many ways, Macleod believed she was a perfect teacher for her. Clarissa could breach that line where you had to force an issue, but she never got caught on the wrong side. Hope would need to know these things. But she could also teach Hope how to play a man, not sexually, but by reaching those parts of him that feel endearment beyond a sexual response. These parts instilled a loyalty that was often undeserved and hard for the man to ignore. Macleod never knew how women did that. And Clarissa did it well. Classy if exuberant, like her car.

Macleod started to move off, but as he was about leave the poolside, he heard a shout from O'Malley.

'Internal, Macleod, trust me.'

Chapter 17

Hope McGrath was sitting in a car racing towards Wick. She had waited out on the A9 while a member from the drug squad down in Glasgow had driven up along with several vans from his team towards Wick, stopping on the way to give Hope a lift. Once in the car, she was briefed on how they were following a fishing boat, which was about to come into Wick Harbour. They believed there to be Semtex on board, and from a similar batch to that which caused the explosion on the coach. The sergeant driving the car was quite enamoured with having Hope on board and talked incessantly all the way to Wick. Hope could smell the egg sandwich on his breath and wondered if it would be impolite to pop to a shop for some mints and then offer them to him.

While his personal hygiene may not have been the best, the sergeant certainly came through with the goods as Hope sat on the harbour side at Wick watching the team storm the boat as soon as it had tied up. Those on board were taken to Wick Police Station and held in the cells while the Glasgow team organised themselves for the subsequent interviews and set up forensic information-gathering around the boat. While the team were getting ready for the interviews, Hope stepped out and found a place to eat. She wondered when next she'd be able to feed her famished stomach. It was still a two-hour drive back to Inverness, and more importantly, back to her vehicle. She wasn't sure when the Glasgow team would be making that trip. As she sat sipping lemonade, her mobile rang, and she picked it up to see the inspector was on the other end of the line.

'Hope, got some information for you. I spoke to O'Malley. He's saying he's not involved at all. He's not even being coy about it, very straightforward, and he makes a lot of sense. I checked with drugs division and his business is good. He doesn't need a lot of territory. Seems quite happy with what he's got. He's old in the tooth as well. Probably a bit wiser than Devine. Certainly doesn't seem the type to start a gang war. He's also disclaiming any idea that he would use Semtex. We checked his history. I can't see any public injury. Everything he's done, he's done to rivals. Everything he's suspected of has the trademark that the public seem to be kept well out of the way. He's keen not to draw too much attention to himself.'

'That old thing, as long as they keep fighting amongst themselves, nobody's that worried. That what you're on about?' asked Hope.

'Exactly. He doesn't leave bodies out in the open. They get buried, the ones he's suspected of killing. Other people have disappeared. He might be a nasty piece of work, but he's a sharp one and he understands public perception and how quick heat can be applied to his operation. Doesn't seem to need to be as brash as Devine. In fact, he dressed a couple of his people down in front of Clarissa.'

'Dressed them down in front of Clarissa?' said Hope,

surprised. 'What did she do to them?'

'She threw them in the pool, Hope. I told you she could handle herself. She doesn't mess about.'

'Were they big guys?' asked Hope.

'Proper big guys. She's old school. She fights dirty. She's not like you with your hand-to-hand techniques. Stomped on their bare feet, handcuffed them, shoved them in the pool. Quick, nasty, effective.'

'Okay, Seoras, but you didn't ring me just to tell me that.'

'No, what's your update?'

Hope explained the situation, and she could hear the silence as Macleod was thinking.

'You'll not be in the interview but stay close to it. Make sure they ask about who that Semtex is going to. I need to know O'Malley's not involved. He might be playing me for the fool. If he is, he's doing it darn well. Find out where it went and don't be afraid to jump in if you have to.'

'That's understood,' said Hope. 'Anything else?'

'It's McGinty's funeral tomorrow. What's your status? Are you going to be down here for it? Might be handy having everyone around. I have a feeling we could get busy soon.'

'I don't know how long it's going to take, Seoras. I'll get the information from up here, make sure I've closed off everything that we need, and then I'll get the first bus, train, or whatever back down.'

'Understood,' said Macleod. 'We're a little bit behind the drag curve here, and I don't like it. I'm missing something. O'Malley said it was an interior job. We know that McGinty caused issues. We know McGinty was a nasty boy, but Devine was happy with him. It's not an easy situation to sort out for anybody further down the chain. Also, an extreme solution to the problem. Were they planting a bomb to give us cover, to make it look like there was somebody else?'

'However it's done, it's done it well,' said Hope. 'We don't seem to be able to trace it to anyone.'

'Until now. Get on that Semtex; find out who it went through. That's going to be our link.'

'Will do, Seoras. Keep safe. By the sounds of it, things are going to heat up.'

Macleod laughed. 'Don't worry. I've got the Urquhart protecting me.'

McGrath smiled as she closed down the phone call. Rising from her table and leaving some cash, she made her way back to the police station where she found that the temporary room set aside for the Glasgow drugs team was awash with activity. Hope ascertained they were about to start interviewing and asked if she could listen in. It was just professional courtesy because otherwise, why was she there? There were five men on board the fishing vessel and all five had to be interviewed.

The first was the master of the vessel, a grizzly old man who said nothing. The next three were younger men. Hope watched her counterparts offer them all sorts of deals to try and get the men to talk. They wanted to know the chain, where the Semtex was coming from. There were also a number of drug packets on board, and much of the afternoon was spent asking where they had come from. By eight o'clock that night, Hope had had enough. It had been a long day, and she was struggling to focus. As the last interviewee came in, she looked at the man before her and wondered had he even begun to shave. He must've been seventeen, maybe eighteen at the most. Then again, there was nobody with him, so he must've been older than he looked. The man refused a lawyer and as

Hope continued to watch, she found him babbling about his girlfriend and the trouble she was going to be in because they had got caught with the shipment.

The sergeant who had driven Hope up that day was running the interview, and almost immediately jumped all over the man. He was agreeing that the man's life could be in danger and offering cooperation as a way out. Clearly, the man didn't trust having a lawyer in either. Hope listened as, over the next thirty minutes, her counterpart managed to secure a deal with the man. He then started spilling the beans.

The fishing boat had been operating in the area for quite a while. On the back of it was stored several drug packages to be dropped off at various harbours around the North Coast. They were also carrying an amount of Semtex for delivery to specified customers. Hope listened as the young man detailed the manifest as they arrived at each port, what had been taken on, and what had been taken off. It was only when he talked about the Semtex being removed in the Banff area, a town east of Inverness, that Hope's ears pricked up. She knocked on the interview door, strode in and asked the sergeant if she could ask a few questions. She saw the young man look at her suspiciously.

'Of course,' said the other sergeant. 'This is DS Hope McGrath,' he explained to the young man. 'She's particularly interested in the Semtex, and what happened to it.'

'You said you dropped it off in Banff. How?' asked Hope.

'There was a man waiting there,' said the man. 'It went in a crate load of fish.'

'Did you recognise him?'

'No, I didn't. I haven't been doing this for long.'

With the deal he negotiated, Hope believed him, but she

continued to press. 'Who did you give it to? What did he look like?'

'He was wearing a cap with a hoodie over it. I couldn't see much from the boat from where I was.'

Hope's heart sank, but she continued to press. 'What can you tell me about him? What did he look like?'

'Well-built, medium.'

'That's nothing. You're just describing the average person. Come on. What did you see? Colour of the cap?'

'Black,' said the man.

'The hoodie?'

'Dark blue.'

'Any other features?' asked Hope, aware that she was now leaning on both her hands, poised over the table at the man, her red ponytail flopping down the side of her shoulder.

'I don't know who he was,' said the man. 'He just came and picked up the stuff.'

Hope thought for a moment then asked, 'Did any of the others say anything about him, give you any name?'

The man looked rather sheepish.

'What did they say?' asked Hope. 'Tell me what they said. You made a deal here. A deal can easily be taken back off the table.' Beside her, the sergeant looked nervous. Hope ignored him, continuing, 'Tell me what you know. Did they say anything else about him?'

'They said to me,' said the young man, 'that he was one of Devine's, whoever he is.'

Hope stood up, turned her back, and started walking around the room. 'Are you sure?' she asked. 'Are you sure he said Devine?'

'Yes, he said Devine. Who the hell's Devine?'

'Did they mention an O'Malley at all?'

'No. Never an O'Malley. It was just Devine, and it was once as we were going away. The master didn't look very happy about him saying it either. Said we don't talk about customers. I think they only knew about him by name, because they had to give it to someone.'

The name's out there, so everybody keeps their mouth shut, thought Hope. *Everybody knows that Devine will come for you if you snitch on him.* She looked across at the man behind the table, who she believed was in a world of trouble.

'Definitely no O'Malley. Is that right?'

The man nodded. 'I told you, Devine. That's all they said, was Devine. Come on. I've told you about everything else. All the drugs, I told you where we dropped them. I'm sorry. I don't know this one. This was out of the ordinary.'

'Why have you still got Semtex on board?'

'Because we're holding it for them in case they need more,' said the man.

'More?' said Hope. 'They were planning more?'

The man raised his shoulders, then put his arms out indicating that he was at a loss. 'I don't know. I have no idea what they were going to do. You don't ask these things on the boat like that. Not without getting thrown over the side.'

Hope nodded, walked over to the sergeant and whispered in his ear that she was done and thanked him. Striding out of the interview room, Hope sat down in the nearest office and called Macleod.

'Seoras, you need to hear this. The shipment was for Devine's crew. Devine's crew picked it up. He's saying it isn't O'Malley.'

'What the earth's going on?' asked Seoras. 'It must be an internal feud, and we're off to a funeral tomorrow. I think I need to take a good look at this gathering. See if we can pick up any intel. Well done, Hope. Get yourself back down here. This time tomorrow, we're going on fraud watch. See who's not genuinely grieving at this funeral.'

'Given the nature of McGinty, sir, I think you'll find yourself falling over the suspects.'

Chapter 18

Macleod opened the door and asked if his team were ready. Ross looked up at him, giving a nod and Macleod thought he looked sharp in his black tie and white shirt. Clarissa had toned down her colours and was also wearing black that befitted a mourner. As she stood up to Macleod, she took hold of his tie and adjusted it.

'I thought at least you would know how to tie one of these,' she said. 'Teach the new guys a lesson.' Macleod gave the barb a short grimace. But as he turned away, he smiled to himself. She was never behind the door speaking to her boss.

When Hope joined them in the room a couple of minutes later, dressed in a smart black suit with a white blouse underneath, the four headed off to the outskirts of Inverness, to a small burial plot. The site had a small chapel, and as they got closer, Macleod could see various unsavoury characters littered around the place. After a funeral car arrived, the coffin holding the remains of Eamon McGinty was taken out and four men carried it inside the chapel.

Funerals were always strange places to be, as no one really knows how to behave. Of course, Macleod had always been used to funerals on Lewis where the entire village would turn out. If your budgie was related in any shape or form to the deceased person, it was able to attend. And yet for all that, and the large numbers at his wife's funeral all those years ago, he had never felt colder. Emotion could bring up a word out of place, or a truth long hidden. As an officer, he knew he was in the right place, but it did not stop him feeling like a vulture.

Macleod told Ross and Clarissa to wait by the vehicle while he and Hope made their way over, towards the chapel. They stood at a polite distance while other mourners arrived, and then he saw another funeral car coming. Devine emerged from it and stood waiting for another car behind him. From the second car emerged Erin McGinty with her face covered by a black veil. She wore a black hat, jacket, and a modest skirt which covered her knees. As she stepped out, she reached back for the hands of two children. From the other side of the car, a man possibly in his twenties with short black hair emerged. He took up a position beside Erin McGinty, and as soon as she moved, he followed her.

Macleod watched as one of McGinty's children suddenly burst into tears. Erin took the boy to one side, consoling him and hugging the child. Macleod felt like a vulture watching this, but what had surprised him was when she stood up and turned to the young man who had got out of the car with her. Erin chastised him heavily. Macleod suddenly realised how nervous the man was as he became stiff and began glancing around with sharp movements.

Devine came over, presumably saying something about being able to help, but Erin seemed cold, brushing him off in a way that no one else did. Devine let it go, at least for the moment, and Macleod reckoned as she was a widow at the moment, at her husband's funeral, Devine would have to show respect out in public.

Together, the party of five made their way into the chapel, and Hope and Macleod followed them towards the rear door. As they went to enter, a large man stepped across in front of them, announcing it was family and friends only.

Macleod recognised the man as one of Devine's goons, but rather than cause a scene, he simply stepped away to the side of the chapel and found a space where he could look in through a window. Hope stood guard in case anyone else approached from the side, but Macleod got a full view of what was happening. Erin McGinty was sitting in the very front row, her two children beside her. Devine was there with his family in the row across, and the young man who had been flanking Erin was sitting behind her. The service was short, brief, and there was no eulogy, the vicar simply giving a few words of consolation.

When the funeral party emerged from the chapel, Macleod watched them take a short walk to the churchyard, less than five hundred metres away. There were a number of people smoking, standing at the side, but as soon as the coffin appeared, they suddenly became a line, flanking the path out to the graveyard. Macleod wondered if this some sort of gang ritual.

The vicar followed the coffin, along with Erin McGinty and her children, up to the gravesite where again, he spoke words of consolation. Macleod was particularly interested when he saw Erin pick up a handful of soil and fling it hard into the grave. Her children did the same. As they stepped back, one by one, the rest of the members of Devine's group came up to pay their respects. Devine was the last, standing over the large hole, looking down at the coffin before making his way over to Erin McGinty. She accepted the consoling hug from him, but in every other respect, she was blatantly ignoring the man.

Macleod stood aloof, having previously advised his people to keep their eyes everywhere and their mouths shut. Today was a day to operate from a distance, not to get involved in some scene. There were newspaper reporters filming every move of the coffin, from its entrance until its descent, but Macleod was not going to appear on any teatime bulletin. When Devine had departed in his funeral car, Macleod slowly made his way over towards Erin McGinty. The young man who was with her stepped forward and Macleod weaved to go past him but found his path blocked.

'I wish to speak to Mrs McGinty,' said Macleod.

'But Mrs McGinty doesn't want to speak to you,' said the man.

'When I hear that from Mrs McGinty, I'll walk.' Macleod tried to brush past him, but the man moved over again. The sneer on the man's face crumbled to that of pain. Hope had stepped up, taken the man's arm, and was very discreetly but effectively lifting it up behind his back to a point when he was wondering if she was going to break it.

'Just stay there like a good boy,' said Macleod, 'I'm going to talk to Mrs McGinty.' As Macleod got closer, the woman recognised him, but she waited for him to approach her. It was only her two kids standing beside her and as Macleod got close, she stepped away to one side, allowing the gravedigger to move in and start filling the grave up.

'I'm sorry to burden you at a time like this,' said Macleod, 'but I need to check if you are okay.'

'Well, no, Inspector, I'm not okay. Have you seen that goon?

He's been put with me for my protection, Devine said. Snake, total snake. I need out, Inspector. You need to get me out.'

'Bide your time,' said Macleod, 'and then just go. Don't be part of the family anymore.'

'Are you no closer to finding who did it?' she asked. With that, she looked back towards the grave of her husband, a tear run down her face and leaned over towards Macleod keeping her voice away from her children. 'He was a bastard, but he was my bastard.'

Macleod couldn't think of anything to say to that, except to simply nod. 'Who's the goon Devine's given to look after you?'

'McGovern, Patrick McGovern,' she said. 'Him and Eamon didn't see eye to eye so I guess that's why Devine's got him with me just in case Eamon's hatched up some plan with me, some sort of pre-meditated revenge. I don't do these gang politics. I don't get involved in it. I hate it. I just want to go somewhere, get away, take these kids out of here.'

Macleod nodded. He understood. 'How often has McGovern been hanging around?'

'Only since Eamon died. Devine's put him on me. I heard there were several other killings as well.'

'There have been, so I'd advise you to stay in the house,' said Macleod.

'I haven't left it, I'm too scared to leave it. Do you understand that, Inspector? I had to order these things online, had to order my funeral clothes online.'

'Has Devine been round?' asked Macleod.

'No. He set Patrick McGovern on me. He's my babysitter to make sure I don't say nothing, but I've got nothing to say. Eamon didn't say anything to me.'

'Well, if you accept, I offer my condolences,' said Macleod.

'Go home and stay safe. We'll be in touch. Hopefully, I can get this wrapped up soon, and you can go off to a different life.' Macleod picked his way back across the burial ground towards Hope, who was still holding McGovern with an arm up his back.

'I heard Devine's put you on watch duty?' McGovern looked slightly surprised.

'Watch duty?'

'Yes. Looking after the merry widow,' said Macleod. For a moment the man looked puzzled, then he nodded. 'Anything happens to her I hold you responsible, and I will come for you,' said Macleod. 'She doesn't need to be a part of any of this. Do you understand?'

The man looked back at her and then nodded to Macleod. 'She'll be all right. I'll look after her. Don't worry.'

'That's what I am worrying about. When Mr. Devine looks after people, they tend to get into trouble.'

'I said I'd look after her, Inspector.' Hope let the man's arm go and he made his way back over to Erin McGinty and her children. Hope and Macleod joined Clarissa and Ross back in the car, but just as Hope was about to drive off, Clarissa called a hold.

'Do you notice something?' she said.

'What?' asked Macleod.

'She's still there, with that guy.'

'That's her protection. He's not going to leave her,' said Macleod.

'No, but she could leave him. She could get in a car, drive home. Why would he stand there? She's been talking to him.'

'How do you mean?' asked Macleod.

'Under breath, angry, I can't read the words, I can't make out

157

what she's saying, but she certainly letting him know a piece of her mind.'

'She's not just a little lady,' said Macleod. 'She might have lived in the shadow of McGinty, but you learn how to be a survivor if you are married to a man like that. She must have had plenty of guys coming round from the crew, as she's a good-looking woman.'

'She's the sort that some men go for, especially the macho types,' said Clarissa. 'They wouldn't be after Hope here—too strong—but that woman, she's got an interior strength but, on the outside, she looks like she can be dominated. Someone like McGinty would get hold of her, to make her comply. Guys like that, if you understand me, see a lot in a woman like that.'

Macleod turned to look at his colleague. 'You think she'd be the dominated little woman? You think McGinty was all over her?'

Clarissa looked. 'No. She's strong. You can see it. She's standing there, nobody's taking her away, nobody else is giving on the orders. She's strong. But she'd play the part for them if it worked for her.'

Macleod nodded and sat back in his seat. He was exhausted because the investigation just seemed to keep meandering. 'I'm buying that one. I'm definitely buying that one,' he said.

Hope started the engine, and together the four departed the funeral wondering if they had seen anything of significant note.

Chapter 19

It took Macleod twenty minutes after returning from the funeral to decide what to do next. Part of him was anxious with what he was about to ask his team to do, but it seemed they could handle themselves. As his team assembled in Macleod's small office around the table, which was often used for conferences, Macleod continued to look out of the window. He swore one day, they would think he was becoming senile because he seemed to stare more and more at the bland landscape in front of him. One day he'd get them to chop down those trees at the far end or at least make a view to the hillside.

'Officers all here, Seoras,' said Hope McGrath, closing the door.

'Good,' said Macleod. 'We need to get a move on. McGinty's been buried. By the looks of it, Devine's got a problem within his organisation. The Semtex was delivered to one of Devine's men, dropped off from a boat in Banff. From there, it was used to blow up the coach. Now someone had a grievance against Eamon McGinty. His wife's running scared. One of our first things is to keep an eye on that situation. Hope, I want you to cover that off. Keep eyes on what's happening between Devine and the McGinty household. See who goes along. Who needs to shut who up. May actually help us figure out who carried out this bombing.'

'Of course, Seoras, going to need a couple of uniform with me, obviously undercover though.'

'Take all you need. Tell the desk sergeant that you have cleared it through me. Not a problem.'

'What about us?' asked Clarissa.

'I want you to start shaking down the lowlifes within the organisation. Find out who his dealers are on the street. Put a bit of pressure on. I need a better picture of it all. I need to understand who McGinty was really up against. I doubt it's Devine. If it was, he wouldn't clear shop. That would also be easy for us to work out what's happened. It's a bit extreme for bringing in a lot of heat over somebody he could have just taken to a back alley and disposed of. This has been done by someone else, possibly to make it look like it's not internal.

'When Devine finds out about the Semtex, discovers it came through an order given by someone pretending it came from his group, he's going to be up in arms. Devine's going to find who used his name to carry out this act. He'll know it's happened because we found out and he has someone leaking to him from within the force. Devine will try and silence whoever picked up the Semtex before we get to them. He'll be worried about a deal being made, his organisation under threat from us. So, Clarissa and Ross, get onto the streets.'

'Work from the bottom up?' asked Clarissa. 'That what you want, Seoras?'

'Exactly. Talk to the drugs section and don't hang about either. Get in, find the information, get it back to me, and make sure you come back, too. This thing is simmering, but with McGinty in the ground, I think Devine is going to act.

He's been biding his time, working out who did it, working out who killed his girlfriend as well. Up until now, he was unsure. Was it his rival? Was it his own people? The Semtex leak, when it happens, will give him the answer.'

'What about Declan O'Malley?' asked Clarissa.

'You heard him,' said Macleod. 'He's keeping out of this. The last thing he wants is to lose a lot of footmen for something he didn't start. Get going.'

Clarissa and Ross stood up, gave the inspector a nod, and left the room. As Hope got up, Macleod came over. He held her hand. 'Just a second. Keep a special eye on Erin McGinty. She's scared. I'm worried somebody could come in and finish her off. Since she's tied to Eamon McGinty, she might know things. One of the rivals has taken out Eamon; it may be because of things he knew, not necessarily to try to move up the ranks. It's a tricky one this, Hope, but I want eyes on and that's why I want you there.'

'Keep in touch, Seoras. I'll let you know if anything happens.'

Macleod turned away and began to look out the window again. He had just moved his pawns. Now we have to see what the enemy reaction would be.

* * *

'What's the big deal about it?' asked Ross, looking at the junkie before him.

The man shook his shoulders. 'I don't want to talk about that. McGinty might be dead, but you don't know who else was with him. These people, they all want to take over. That's the problem. There's no chain of command like there used to be. That used to be Mr. Devine. If the word came down from Mr. Devine, that was that, but McGinty was off just here, there, and wherever imposing his own will. I'm not sure he even told the boss at times.'

'You got to give me more than that,' said Ross. 'We've just listened to you but you're sitting there with how much white stuff in your pockets? We could put you away for a good while but I don't want you. You're nothing. I want the big dogs.'

'You can't do this to me, man.' The man was pulling his jacket up around him, his face gaunt, the neck tight, and Ross could see him sweating. He was unsure if it was because he needed to use or if he was simply panicking by the idea of a prison sentence. The smell did not help Ross either, the man clearly having never seen a washbasin, never mind a bath, in quite a while.

'This time they'll take me down proper. It won't a brief stay. At the start they try and get you better, but you don't so after a while they give up. They just throw away the key. That's where I'm going. You can't take me in.'

Clarissa stepped forward, her foot on the man's toes. 'Then you need to come up with something. Otherwise, that's exactly what I'm doing. I'm taking you in. In fact, I'm taking you in any way.'

'No, no,' said the man. 'No, no. Look, I'll introduce you to some people. Okay? If you want to know, then I need to take you to some people who do know. I'm nothing. You understand that, don't you? I just ship a bit of this stuff out, get people smacked up, take a bit of it myself. I'm bottom chain here, bottom feeder dragged along the ocean floor. Now you need the guy at the top, well, at least the guy above me. Let me make a phone call.'

'You've got a minute,' said Clarissa, 'and I'm listening.'

The man nodded and pulled out a mobile phone. After ten seconds, he spoke and a gruff voice replied, 'As long as it's a friend, yes, meet us in the bar. You know where.

The phone call ended as abruptly as it began, making Clarissa wonder exactly what had been agreed. The man started to walk away. 'Come on,' he said. 'It's not far. I'll take you in and you can have words with him. It's not coming from me because I don't know anything.'

The man moseyed along, Clarissa quite agitated behind him. The pair of officers walked a small distance behind the man and Ross looked across at Clarissa.

'You sure we should be doing this?'

'Seoras said to push the buttons. Just watch your back and mine too.'

'We could be heading into anything,' said Ross.

'Of course, but we need to force something. Something's got to give. We're getting nowhere. Come on. Stay close by.'

The pair followed the man around several street corners and into a back alley. At the end of it was a single metal door which he rapped on lightly. It swung open. The officers were led into a dark room which then broke into a small concert room with a stage on one side. As he entered, Ross could hear the door being closed behind them. At first, the man turned around and just stood there before calling on Dicky. Dicky emerged; a squat man, balding, with a cigarette in his mouth.

'What's this then?' said Ross. 'Is this the guy we want to talk to?'

'I'm here to talk to you,' said the guy. 'Who's coming poking their nose in. I don't care if you're an officer. We can't have anything blowing up at the moment. They took him out, didn't they? They took out McGinty. What did he do?'

'As far as I know,' said Ross, 'he did nothing. Now, why are we here if you're not going to tell me anything?'

'You're right; I'm not going to tell you anything, cop. We can't have you snooping around either.' Ross heard something behind him. Both he and Clarissa turned to look, seeing three more men walk into the room. One held a baseball bat and the other two knives. On returning his gaze to the front, the bald man had pulled out a butterfly knife while the junkie wandered over to the bar to collapse against it.

'End of the line,' said the man. 'Somebody's been into our group. Somebody has been coming in, getting information. Don't like coppers who sneak like this, coming in from underneath. Something's wrong with you two. Not for long though. They won't know where you've been, will they? They'll never find your bodies either.'

Clarissa ignored the man at the front and kept her gaze upon the three men coming towards her. The one with the baseball bat took the lead. As he stepped up towards her, he pointed it holding it in one hand, right in her face. The other two men took up flanking positions.

'Just take it easy, everybody. There's no need for this,' said Ross. 'We can walk away from this. You don't need to be murderers because they'll come for you. Police officers—they'll hunt you down; you know that.

'Nobody's going to hunt me down,' said the man with the baseball bat. With a flick, he pushed it right at Clarissa's face.

Stepping to one side, Clarissa grabbed the baseball bat with one hand, while her other free hand reached inside her jacket pocket, took out a pepper spray and hit the man right in the face between the eyes. By the time he reached up with his hands to his eyes, Clarissa had taken away the baseball bat and had planted it in the face of the guy next to her. The third guy moved forward and she caught him on the arm with the bat. He spun around, came at her again but she cracked him on top of the head.

The man who had been pepper sprayed shook his head, trying to clear his streaming eyes, and charged blindly at her. She took the end of the bat and rammed it right in between his legs, causing him to bowl over. As he hit the ground, she hit him again on the back with the bat. The man at the front with the knife made a dart towards Ross, but he stepped to one side, catching the man with a kick to the knee. The man spun around, the knife still ready, only to be flattened by a blow from the baseball bat into the side of his head.

'Don't get up,' said Clarissa. 'Anybody moves, you'll not move again.'

Ross looked around them, fighting to control his disbelief. He bent down beside one of the men lying on the floor.

'Who was it? Who was after Eamon McGinty? Tell me.'

There was silence from the beaten bodies apart from the occasional groan. Clarissa smacked the baseball bat on the floor. She watched the junkie who had brought them in jump suddenly. She made her way over to him, grabbing him by the shirt collar, throwing him on the floor in between the four men.

'Five of you, jumping us,' she said. 'If you want to walk out of here alive, I want you to talk right now.'

'You can't do that,' said Ross. 'You can't threaten them like that. It won't stand.'

'I'm not looking for it to stand. I just want answers. Now you,' said, Clarissa pointing the baseball bat in the face of the man who attacked her with it, his eyes were still streaming

165

with tears from the pepper spray, 'you tell me who was after McGinty.'

'Clarissa, he needs an ambulance. We'll get back up and—'

Clarissa slammed the baseball bat on the floor again. 'Not for these, no, we won't. We need to know who was it? Who did it? Tell me now; otherwise, I start breaking legs.'

Chapter 20

'Dermot Fudge,' said Clarissa before awaiting Macleod's response to see if he knew the man. 'Did you have any trouble getting the information?'

'Not a problem, sir. I was just a bit shocked at how intimidating I can be.'

'As long as you were by the book.'

'They attacked us, jumped us, so yes. They tried to murder us, sir, so I was by the book. I gave them hell back.'

Clarissa could hear Macleod's teeth crunching but all he said back was, 'Good. Go find him. See what's happening.'

When Clarissa put the phone down, she turned to see Ross looking at her. 'What?'

'You said you were going to kill them.'

'And what? They just tried to murder us. It was more convincing. They took us away to a place where nobody was and nobody knew and we turned around and beat them up. I thought dumping a little fear back on them might help considering the fact we were never taking them in.'

'I didn't like it,' said Ross. 'It's not how Macleod would have done it.'

'Your inspector's a dirtier fighter than you know. When the chips are down, he fights just like me.'

Ross wasn't so convinced, but he drove the car back to the station where the pair of them had a word with the drugs section, picking up addresses where Dermot Fudge could possibly be.

'He seems to be a man with needs,' said Ross.

'Why do you say that?'

'Clarissa, look. Those addresses, that one, that one, and that one. They've all been labelled as brothels. The other ones, those flats are women-only. I'm sure it's one of those buildings by the college. You're not meant to be in there as a man, or at least under certain restrictions. Yet, he seems to be tagged for them all. That'd be a man that likes to spread his cash around and get favours in return.'

'He shouldn't be too hard to track down then, should he?' said Clarissa. As she marched out of the station, she flung her scarf around her neck. Then, it occurred to her that this would be the work she'd be taking on, no longer following arts around the world, but instead chasing up dirty perverts in brothels.

The first address they arrived at looked very much like an ordinary house, and Clarissa insisted that Ross knock on the door. A small eye-hatch pulled back. A woman looked out before the door opened fully. She was dressed in a neat suit and asked Ross what he wanted. He told her he was there for the four o'clock. The woman brought him in, but when she went to close the door, Clarissa put a foot in it and forced it open as well.

'Hey, what's this?'

'We're here for Dermot Fudge. Is he about?' Clarissa flashed her warrant card.

'I haven't seen Dermot in days. Not after, well, Eamon McGinty.'

'After McGinty? What's the deal with McGinty?' asked Clarissa, pretending she didn't know.

'The bomb. He's the one that got blown up in the bomb. But even then, Dermot Fudge was rarely around here. He used to be, all the time. Then McGinty came around, but I'm glad he's gone. Some of the girls, they really didn't like him. I mean, you're used to some of these guys being a bit rough, but not like McGinty. McGinty was brutal, and he didn't like Dermot. They didn't see eye to eye, so Dermot didn't come back. The girls liked Dermot, though. Big tipper. Not a bad guy to be with, either.'

'You don't mind if I don't trust you and actually search the place?' said Clarissa, making her way up the stairs.

'There's clients in up there. You can't just barge in,' said the woman. Clarissa ignored her and Ross watched the scarf stream out behind her as Clarissa bolted up the stairs. Arriving at the first door, she threw it open, put her head in to see a pair of white buttocks gyrating. Clarissa walked over, grabbed the man's hair and turned his head towards her. 'No, not this one,' she said.

As she was leaving the room, the man started shouting at her saying what he would do to her. Clarissa stopped, turned on her heel and looked at the man. 'Detective Sergeant Urquhart. Now, shut up or I'll book you.'

The man's face went white but Clarissa didn't hang about, marching off to the next room to find that Ross had already joined her on the landing. The next one had a similar picture, as with the other five, but Dermot Fudge was nowhere in the building. The mistress of the house was in an uproar.

'Look, love, don't get upset,' said Clarissa, 'because if I want, I can put the call in and they'll bust this place now. Because there's so much hassle, these guys will not come back. Am I understood?'

The woman nodded slowly. 'But he's not here. Dermot's not here.'

'Where is he then? Give me some numbers, addresses.' The woman reluctantly wrote down on a piece of paper several of the addresses that Ross and Urquhart already had. The pair set off in their car again, checking on each address and finding a similar picture. It was only when they got to the flats of female-only occupants that they got a better idea of what was going on. When they knocked on the door of a young girl who Clarissa reckoned was only nineteen, they were rather alarmed to see that there were photographs of Dermot Fudge on the wall. The girl sat on a chair while Clarissa pulled up a stool in front of her.

'You and Dermot Fudge are an item then?' asked Clarissa. The girl nodded but her eyes were starting to water, tears beginning to flow.

'He's gone underground, hasn't he?' said the girl. 'He's worried about people coming for him after what happened to that guy on the coach.'

'The coach happened to a lot of people, actually,' said Ross. 'Who specifically?'

'McGinty. He used to talk about McGinty all the time in his sleep. He was obviously bothered by him. I used to have to try and calm him down, rub his shoulders, his neck, but McGinty was always on his mind. Then he was happy,' she said, 'happy

McGinty was dead. But now the fingers have been starting to point, people asking who did it. He said to me they should be looking at the other side, the rivals across town, the Irish mob, but no. Some of them were looking at him. He couldn't handle it, so he's gone to ground. You'll never find him.'

'It's not me finding him I'm worried about,' said Clarissa; 'it's somebody else finding him.'

* * *

Macleod walked along the street in front of Erin McGinty's house, and further up, he could see a car he recognised. Hope was watching as he'd asked her to and when he'd given her a call, she had said all had been quiet with only Mrs McGinty in the house. Her guard had left a half hour earlier, but Hope was unsure if he was coming back. So far, Devine and none of his other goons had turned up, so maybe Mrs McGinty was in the clear. Maybe Devine knew she didn't have anything to pass on. Macleod wanted to talk to the woman to see if she knew any more about McGinty's rivals within the gang.

He climbed up onto the front steps, rapped the door, and then stepped down again waiting. It was two minutes before the door opened. Mrs McGinty, wrapped in a large towel bathing robe, looked down at the Inspector.

'Sorry to bother you, ma'am, but I need to talk.'

'You don't want to be here, to see me. You're lucky they're out because otherwise—but then again—'

'I understand you're anxious, worried.'

'I'm not worried, I'm scared, I am terrified,' she said. 'If they know you've been here without anyone listening, they'll be thinking I'm telling you stuff.'

'But that's what I want. I want you to tell me stuff. Eamon, what happened with him? Who was his enemy? Why was he struggling within the group?'

'That's the trouble, isn't it?' she said. 'Eamon made waves. Eamon was on the rise and a lot of them couldn't handle it. A lot of them saw themselves as the next successor to step up into the number two spot for Devine. But Eamon was going to take that, and he started shoving everyone out of the way. That's why it's come back at him. I mean even here; I've got Patrick McGovern looking after me.'

'The man who was out at the funeral?'

'That's right. Devine won't let him go away. In fact, he's only just been called back for some reason. That's the thing, Inspector, I'm trapped here.'

'If you let it go, you might come out the other side,' said Macleod. 'Just wait it out. Bide your time. Let us arrest who did do this, then get out.'

'But there's no time. Inspector, you must understand that. How can I live amongst these gangsters?'

'You're also being protected,' said Macleod. 'You're being watched, the gangsters are being watched, but you've also got protection. Devine doesn't want anything to happen to you so he's got McGovern here.'

'Don't talk to me about that. McGovern, he's not what he seems. He's not just a daft lad. You have to understand that he terrifies me because the last time we were alone he, well, he took me. You understand me, Inspector?'

Macleod did only too well and noticed a loss of confidence in the woman's eyes. 'That's what I live with, that threat again, and he used it. He said several times what he'll do to me if I don't comply. I need out. You understand that, Inspector, I need out.'

'You shall get out. I'll take you now into protective custody if you want.'

'That wouldn't be any sort of protection from this lot. At least when Eamon was here, I had some sort of protection even if he wasn't much of a man himself, always so angry.'

'If McGovern has done this before, why did you never tell Eamon?'

'Because he wouldn't believe me, and then I'd be a smoking pile of ash as well.' Macleod nodded. He looked around the room. There were pictures of Eamon McGinty with his boys everywhere.

'He would protect me, but if I said to him that McGovern had done something he'd probably have snapped, decided that I was at fault as well. He wasn't a stable man in that sense. Can you get that, Inspector, and get why I didn't do anything, why I've had to bide my time?'

'You'll have to bide it some more,' said Macleod, 'unless you're telling me someone's threatening you. If you tell me, I can get you out.'

'And what? You'll stick me in a refuge somewhere for them to find me? No, I need you to solve this case. I need you to find who did this, so things will settle down and I'll be left alone. I can sit and do my year or two. Sit here and show them I have nothing to give to anyone else, that I don't know anything. Devine can satisfy himself that I'm no risk, and I'll move on and get my children a life.'

Macleod nodded, gave a sigh, and turned as if to leave. 'What would you have done if Eamon had managed to displace Devine? Would you have stayed with him?' asked Macleod, 'Because to be honest, from what you've told me, you didn't really want to be here with him.'

'Look at me, what could I have done? If it's not Eamon, it just becomes the next one, doesn't it? It just becomes the one that replaces him. You don't have a standing as a woman amongst these people; they'll just take. Eamon told me that. Told me I was fortunate. He told me about Maggie Brown, how she'd had gone over to Devine. He said she was lucky that O'Malley let her leave because Devine, he basically took her over; he gave her no option.'

'Maybe that's why O'Malley let her go.'

'Oh, he's the same as the rest. Don't fool yourself, Inspector. All these people, they're all the same but they never get what's coming to them. It's always some other poor bugger. You know, they killed Eamon. I've got boys without a father now. What good does that do? Not that he was much of a role model for them anyway. I need to be away. I need to have a proper life, but I need to be safe in it. Do you get that, Inspector?'

Macleod sighed again. 'That's something that's not guaranteed to any of us. My advice would be to stay put, ride out the storm, then move when nobody's interested in you, but if you're under threat now, I will take you in.'

'They'll see that as a betrayal. They'll see that I've got some information to give and any arrest that follows will be on me. Sacrifice my children. No, Inspector. This is my place to stay. Eamon made that very, very obvious.'

'Do you want my card?' asked Macleod. 'You can ring me any time.'

The woman refused. 'I don't want anything of you here. Now, go before McGovern comes back.'

'Who do you think killed your husband? A colleague of mine thinks Dermot Fudge might be involved.'

'He did have problems with Eamon. Eamon talked about him a lot. They didn't see eye to eye. Eamon was bypassing him. At least that's as much as I could gather.' Macleod thought that she seemed to be very au fait with the group considering she wasn't happy being amongst it.

'But Eamon talked. You have to understand that, Inspector. I'm not just here to bring up the kids. They all want someone to talk to, someone on which to unburden, and they can't talk to any of the rest of them because they'd all betray each other in a flash. They tell you everything and you suffer in that way as well.'

As Macleod was walking away, he caught the hand on his shoulder and turning around, Erin McGinty looked up at him, her hands almost shaking. 'Beware of Patrick McGovern. He's, well, he's—'

'He's what?' asked Macleod.

'He's not here without reason. I can't tell you more. Just beware of him. I don't know for sure, but he's been controlling since he's been here. He's happy doing things, hiding stuff, and I can't say any more, but you need to go. He'll be here soon. If you're here, it'll be bad for me. You need to go, Inspector, but just keep an eye on him.'

Macleod was ushered along the path, but rather than look for more, he began his walk back to his car. As he strode along, something in his mind was ticking. The whole picture was cloudy, but bits and pieces would reveal themselves. All he had to do was wipe away the rest of the cloud. As he reached his car, he received a phone call.

'Sir, it's Clarissa. We've found Dermot Fudge.'

Chapter 21

In the darkness of night, Macleod watched the brothel house, a rather plain building set at the end of an industrial park. The street it was located on ran along to a small retail park and the house was a bit of an anomaly. It seemed to Macleod it had been there from an earlier time while everything else was built around it. It clearly would not be a building you would want for your own house, but in the meantime, it had been put to good use, or at least that's how those running that sort of business would view it.

Clarissa and Ross had spent the time interviewing suspects but Macleod had been sitting on the car bonnet, staring blankly up at the house, his mind whirling away. On arrival, he had traipsed up the stairs into a small room with pink furnishing and the body lying on the bed. There were cuts, deep and gaping, bruises from where the man had been beaten with something, but the sickening sight was the open stomach and the internal organs lying on the bed. Clarissa had looked the worse for wear and Macleod reckoned she had disappeared somewhere to vomit, and he certainly didn't blame her. It was one of the goriest things he had witnessed but unfortunately, not one that he had failed to see before. Back in Glasgow, he remembered some of the turf wars there had ended up with the most horrific beatings and killings of those from rival gangs.

From a professional point of view, one of the most interesting patterns about the brothel was the fact that everyone who was there seemed keen to tell you who their client had been and what they'd been doing. Normally when these sorts of places were raided everyone denied all knowledge of being there; 'Just passing through and why am I dressed like this? Well, it just happened to be a rough night.' Instead, the entertaining women were keen to furnish numbers of who had been with them and those who had been caught or already there were more than happy to describe their entertainment and how it clearly meant that they couldn't have been in the room when the man died. *This would be it*, thought Macleod. Someone happily dispatched, no details, no witnesses, nothing. It had Devine's fingerprints all over it. Jona Nakamura approached the Inspector and he stood up off the car, giving her a little smile as she approached.

'Well, it's not been easy,' said Jona, 'due to the amount of damage done to the man but I have identified him. It is Dermot Fudge.'

'Blast!' said Macleod. 'Devine's cleaning house. He's hunting down but there's nothing to say it was Fudge. There's nothing for him to justify this killing.'

'I know I don't work on your side,' said Jona, 'but I wasn't that aware that they justified all their misdeeds.'

'No, Jona, you have to understand that sometimes they do. What's the point of wiping everyone out if you've got a rat on your side? You need to find the rat because then you're still left with a lot of good people who know that if they ever rat on you, you'll come for them big style, and you'll get them. If all they're thinking is, if something happens, you're coming for everyone, why would you have any sort of loyalty to that person? You could be dead through no fault of your own. But Devine's shaken at the moment. He lost his woman. I don't think he's thinking clearly.'

'I better get back in, Inspector. There are some pieces to tidy up but I don't think we're going to get much from the room. You know what these guys are like, clean up afterwards, no traces left, just a handy picture for anyone else who needs to know.' Macleod nodded and followed Jona back into the building, giving a quick look around the ground floor. He managed to spot Hope and give her a nod of the head to indicate she should follow him back out to the car. As he resumed his position on the bonnet, he watched her emerge, and he thought she looked very fresh-faced. The partner she had now was doing her good. Before, he used to see a tautness in her expression, especially when cases were getting to the rough end, but there was a light in her, one he was delighted to see.

'You wanted to see me, boss?'

'What do you think?'

'Like in general, or just about this?'

'Start with this,' said Macleod. 'What do you think of what happened here?'

'It's Devine, isn't it? Devine's come for him.'

'Well, yes, but most of my constables around here could hazard that guess. But why? What's he doing?'

'Well, it seems a bit strong. We have no evidence that Dermot Fudge planted that bomb. Every move that has been made behind this seems to be based on a leak about what we find out. He's either taken the guy to one side and beaten him to a pulp to find out, he's confessed, so he's finished him off completely, or Devine's making a statement.'

'Or—' prompted Macleod.

'Or he's gone a bit wild after the killing of his woman.'

'That's where I am,' said Macleod. 'Never underestimate the rage a man feels when he's lost his partner.' Macleod was thinking back to a time when he lost his own wife and the anger that was inside, albeit, he didn't go to the nearest hoodlum and gut them.

'Bit like a woman scorned, is it?' asked Hope.

'Very much so, possibly even more,' said Macleod, 'but if he's doing this and he's going wild, we need to get a hold of him and we need to make sure he isn't doing it to anyone else.'

'Easier said than done,' said Hope. 'I take it the drug squad will have some way of keeping tabs on him?'

'Already asked them to,' said Macleod, 'but it's not easy. These guys know how to move about, keep off the radar. It's what they do.'

'But if everyone's seen this,' said Hope, 'they'll run, won't they?'

'No,' said Macleod. 'Why run? If you run, he thinks you're guilty. If you don't run, you might be all right. They'll stay very quiet and very low but not run.'

'I take it Clarissa and Ross didn't get a name of who picked up that package, brought the Semtex down from Wick?'

'No,' said Macleod. 'I wish they did because that's either our bomber or somebody very close to them. But this,' said Macleod pointing to the house, 'this is not our killer. This is an angry crime boss. I don't know how I'm going to pin it on him outside of a confession. The man will be well versed on how to do this.'

'Who's in the picture?' said Hope.

'Anyone from Devine's gang who had a grudge against Eamon McGinty. It's certainly not a gang war. Thankfully, Devine has realised that. I'm still surprised at O'Malley though, very calm about Frank Egg.'

Macleod gave a nod and Hope turned round to see Ross exiting the building and coming over. The man looked tired, no doubt after endless interviews, but he was clutching paper in his hand as well as a pen.

'You're not going to believe this, Inspector, but I've gone through everyone, twice after you commented before. Everyone's got an alibi. More than that, we haven't got an alibi from one person which you would suspect, being a brothel, you know? Woman, guy, you'd expect the two of them to be there. They've got alibis to three, four, five people. They weren't even all in the room. They were in other rooms, but they popped in, they looked out, they saw this. The alibi mill has been on full tilt.'

'Now, that's not surprising is it?' said Macleod. 'Would you want to take the rap for this one? They also don't want to get in the way. They'll know Devine's done this. Then what? You end up getting hauled into it, start to blab about something? No, these people are just desperate to keep out of this and I don't think we'll shake them down either. You're talking about their lives on the line. They'll happily take a prostitution rap.' Macleod looked wistfully into the air, then saw a figure approaching from the house. It was an older woman, maybe seventy, approaching with a cane, looking rather smart in a suit. Macleod gave Ross a questioning look.

'That's the manager of the brothel,' said Ross. 'Quite

indignant she can't get back to work.' Macleod nearly burst out laughing. If it hadn't for the seriousness of the crime, he would have shaken his head in despair.

'How long are your people going to be here?'

'As long as they need to,' said Macleod. 'If you go hiring out your rooms for this sort of thing, you're going to have to take the consequences of the police being around.'

'Well, I want you gone. I have a business to run.'

'Excuse me?' said Macleod. 'A business?'

'Indeed, it's all legit and above board. We simply provide services for many lonely men, so kindly get done and get out of here.'

Macleod got up off the car, walked towards the woman, and stared down at her. She was some three inches smaller than he. 'We will be here until we don't need to be here. You, however, will be explaining how legitimate all of this is to some colleagues of mine. This is a coverup for Devine. I know that; you know that; the least you could do is have the decency to play along and stay out of the way, but no, you come and hassle me, and because of that my friends are coming down. Your paperwork better be in order.'

The woman stared back up at him, gave a tut, and then marched off.

'You know she's going to pull that paperwork out, don't you, Seoras?' said Hope.

'Yes, but I will enjoy the hassle of it. She will be running around, covering up and I will enjoy the fact that she'll be cursing my name for doing it to her. Now, we need to start thinking about what we're going to do. Erin McGinty was highlighting Patrick McGovern as a potential threat. He could be our bomber, but I don't really know that much about him.

181

He's certainly sticking close to her.'

'Is he worth checking out then, so we start looking at addresses, haunts, doctor, drug squad, see if they've got anything on him?'

'Yes,' said Macleod, 'because I want to get to him and find out what he knows before Devine gets to him and kills him for no good reason. He's our priority. Are we far away from being finished up here, Ross?'

'Well, Jona will still be here for a bit with her team, but in terms of interviews, we're all done, drawing a blank as you'd expect.'

'Fine,' said Macleod, 'do me a favour, Ross. Call back to the station. See if somebody wants to come down and investigate illegal sex services operating in that house. Somebody pernickety, someone—'

'McCullough?' asked Ross.

Hope spun on her heel looking at Ross. 'Yes,' she laughed, 'McCullough.'

McCullough was one of the most efficient persons Macleod knew and he did everything to avoid working with him. If there wasn't a dot on the I, or a cross on the T, McCullough would find it. He would go on and on about it, wittering away in your ear. The man was a pain; he was perfect for this.

'McCullough, Ross, make sure you tell him that we all have suspicions. Should keep our lady friend in there occupied for at least a couple of days.'

'Once you've done that, get Clarissa and meet us back at the station,' said Hope. 'The boss and I will speak to drugs, work on an action plan for following up on McGovern.'

'Oh, and, Ross,' said Macleod, 'tell McCullough I was thinking of just doing this myself, going the whole hog with the illegal sexual activity. It should get him here in no time.'

'He certainly won't want anyone else taking any credit.' Ross almost skipped back to the house.

As they got into the car, Hope turned on the ignition, but then stopped and looked at her boss. There was something about him at the moment. On one side there was a jovialness, a delight of getting one up on a woman who had been hassling him from the brothel, but Hope was able to see underneath, and the mind was whirring. Often Macleod knew what he was doing, who he was following, who to be on top of, but the man was struggling today.

'Keep churning it over, Seoras. I've never known you not get there in the end.'

'But you haven't worked with me that long, Hope. Some days you get the ones you just don't win.'

Hope watched him look out of the window, expecting a forlorn look, but instead, it was a little grin. Maybe the game was afoot. Maybe he was being tested by someone else and enjoying the challenge. Something was stirring with Macleod.

Chapter 22

Hope glanced down to the address of her list, searching for the next one on the pad, before starting the car again. She was sore. They'd been up all night sorting out their plans. Then first thing in the morning, the hunt for McGovern had started. Hope had taken the addresses on the west side of the town and was to give each location a thorough observation, hopefully not causing the man to run if she did find him. The last house Hope had checked had been easy to peer into, a ground floor flat. She had swung around it, gazing into windows, and when she'd been stopped by a neighbour asking what the hell she was up to, Hope had stood there, asking if McGovern was about.

'I need to speak to him urgently,' she said.

The man opposite her looked her up and down. 'You something to him?'

Hope had put her hand down to just below her belly. 'I'm about to be a lot to him,' she said, 'but I can't get him. He needs to know.'

'Cigar in the post moment, is it?' said the man. 'Congratulations, but I haven't seen him here in days.'

Hope had nodded and left, satisfied McGovern wasn't about, but something had stirred in her when she pretended to be pregnant. Sitting in the car now, she had thoughts of her partner back in his flat that overlooked the sea. She forced the feeling from her mind. There was work to do.

The car was started and Hope drove a short distance to her next stop. It was more awkward, the flat at the top of a small block of ten. There was no way to look in the window without grappling gear coming down from the roof. Hope made her way up the steps inside. She was also aware that the man would have nowhere to run so this was a highly unlikely spot for him to choose. You couldn't jump out of the window without breaking your legs in a fall. She reached the top of the concrete steps that comprised the rather drab interior of the set of flats. Hope saw number ten, an apple green door. She rapped it hard and then stood back, waiting to see who would come.

The door opened and a man stood in a rather disgusting flannel dressing gown. It had once been white but now only the deepest of cleaning fluids would ever see that white again. Hope could see egg stains, possibly a beer, maybe a cup of tea. Everything was on it. The man who was currently occupying the dressing gown was wearing a pair of boxer shorts that were too small for him, and a vest that had ridden halfway up his belly. He was also wearing black socks inside a pair of slippers. Hope wondered if the man was in some way distressed.

'Oh, yes,' said the man. 'Well, how old are you?'

'I'm looking for McGovern,' said Hope.

'Well, he's not here,' said the man. 'You can come in and check if you want. One of his bits on the side, are you? I know he has a few.'

185

Hope strolled into the room, brushing the man to one side, and she could feel him staring at her. Maybe he was one of those men who just didn't get out, had no social scene. He certainly didn't know how to behave towards a woman.

'Very tidy. So which club did he find you in?' asked the man. 'You shaking that booty at him?'

Hope turned around, reached inside her jacket pocket, and shoved her warrant card and badge in the man's face.

'A copper? He picked up a copper. Wow.'

Hope shook her head causing her ponytail to flap around her neck, which only seemed to make the man more excited.

'You, sit down on the sofa, and you give me as much as a passing remark about how I look, and you're coming down the station with me.'

'You could take me anywhere.'

Hope shook her head again. The sooner she got this done, the better, and so she strolled through into the kitchen unit looking around for any hidey holes. She next checked the bedroom, a second bedroom, and the toilet area but there was no one here. Hope walked back out, turned to the man who sat in his flannel dressing gown, and asked, 'When was the last time you saw McGovern?'

'To be honest, it's been days . . . well no, weeks.'

'Does he stay here much?'

'Not really. He usually brings a girl with him, stays the night, and then disappears the next day. He pays for all of this, I don't.'

'So, what? This is his pad away from everyone else? Does anybody else he worked for know about it?'

'Who does he work for?' asked the man. Hope stared trying to ascertain if the guy was genuine, but it seemed he was and if so, wouldn't that be perfect. Working for someone like Devine, you needed to have the ability to vanish in case something happened, and here he had a guy completely separate, but McGovern hadn't been that clever because the drugs unit had managed to find this address, so at some point, they had followed him here.

'Well, thank you for your time.' As Hope went to leave, the man called out at her, and she turned to face him again. He'd stood up now, and was simply looking at her.

'Thank you,' he said, and she realised what he'd just done.

'If I had time, I'd be booking you. You ever touch yourself in front of a woman again, and I'll take it off for you.'

She turned on her heel and walked out. Part of her wondered where this confidence was coming from. Although she knew she could attract men, and she liked to be sought after, Hope had never been one to take on the perverts, dress them down, put them in their place. There was always a lingering doubt about herself, a crazy warrior about her own looks. Maybe it was her new partner, for he wasn't fanciful about her. He wasn't demanding, rather, he was just there. *Maybe that's it*, she thought, making her way down the steps. By the time she got into the car, she was smiling again. Hope completed the rest of her addresses within the next hour and called back into the station.

'I'm going to wilt away in here shortly. Have you heard anything?' Macleod must have been getting anxious for he was not so forceful normally.

'Nothing, drawn a blank.'

'That's not surprising with what's going on. I'd have been going deep underground, places I haven't been before. I reckon he's well out of the way, if he hasn't run. Probably means he's on a train south, or headed to the far north. I guess it's time we put out a proper all person's on him, see if anybody out there in a car can spot him.'

'Agreed,' said Hope. 'If he runs, at least it's running. Easier to see a man on the move than a man tucked up tight.'

'True,' said Macleod. 'That's if he's still around. I'll get that on the way.'

The afternoon was long. Macleod received reports about where Devine was but nothing on McGovern. Maybe McGovern was still in McGinty's house, too scared to leave. Macleod started to get agitated. He didn't have anything. He had nearly thirty-five people dead and he didn't have anything. Why? Somebody was good at this.

Hope burst into the room nearly knocking the door off its hinge and slammed her hands down on Macleod's desk. 'Seen him. Local supermarket, but he's on the run.'

'Have they still got him in sight?' asked Macleod, standing up, then making his way round to grab his coat.

'As far as I know,' said Hope. Macleod was out the door before Hope had a chance, but he shouted across the office at Ross and Clarissa to get moving. The inspector was sitting in the passenger seat, ready to go before Hope had slid in behind the wheel.

If there was half a chance, and we find him, it could be the breakthrough, thought Macleod. He forced himself not to shout at Hope to go quicker. At the end of the day, the uniform car that was after McGovern would keep a tail.

'He's heading into town at the moment,' said Hope looking down at her phone.

'Watch the road. Give me that,' said Macleod. Checking Hope's device, Macleod watched fast text messages keep updating, allowing him to know exactly where McGovern had gone. He had made his way across to the train station running through to the other side. He was now heading across the car park of a large supermarket chain. Hope was close to it and spun the car in the front entrance only to see McGovern jump across and run into where the petrol station was situated on Hope's right-hand side. She continued ahead then turned right, entered the station only to see somebody step out of a black car, grab McGovern and haul him inside.

The petrol station had an entrance in and another one out, both rather narrow sections of road. The car drove past the pumps, took a right, and was going to come out of the exit, but Hope put the brakes on, reversed her car across where the black car was now heading. Macleod looked and waited for the fleeing car to stop, but it didn't. It hammered right into their own car causing it to spin. Macleod was jostled. He turned to see if Hope was okay, but she was already trying to turn the car around to follow the escaping car which was now heading along the main road out of Inverness. As she spun the wheel, the car was uncontrollable and she couldn't get it to move in a straight line. Pulling over to one side, now that the escaping car was well out of sight, Macleod joined her and saw that the rear wheels were so badly damaged the car couldn't go straight.

'No,' shouted Hope. 'No.'

'Number plate,' said Macleod, 'did you get the number plate?' Hope rattled it off to him and Macleod got hold of his phone and called into the station to broadcast the news of the new car they were after. Five minutes later, as they stood at the roadside, Ross pulled up and Macleod got into the car beside him, Hope jumping into the rear.

'Car has just been picked up,' said Ross, 'An industrial estate on the way out. Come on.' It was less than three minutes later that Ross was approaching a large warehouse where a police cordon was being set up.

As they pulled up to the constable standing behind his police car, Macleod jumped out and shouted across at the officer, 'What's the hold-up? Why aren't we going in?'

'Waiting for backup, sir.'

'But that's an execution,' said Macleod, 'they've come for him.' With that, he began to run towards the building, followed by Hope and Ross. The building was at least five hundred metres away and Macleod was quickly overtaken by Hope. On reaching the door, she stepped to one side, opened it before peering in quickly, and then made her way inside.

'Better that they run,' said Macleod who then started shouting, 'Police! Come out, police!' There was the sound of scattering feet, people running downstairs and as Hope made her way up one flight, she charged into one of the men, bouncing him off the wall as she continued to go upwards. Macleod found himself having to step over the man who had a cut on one side of the head after the collision with Hope, but he wasn't going anywhere. Together, they reached the top and burst onto an open floor where in the middle of the dull concrete McGovern was bound, and sitting on a chair.

Someone was lifting him up by the hair. It appeared that his feet had just been cut loose. McGovern was thrown to his knees and Macleod saw the axe being brought out. By God, they were actually going to behead him. Hope raced forward, seeing the man lift the axe. Clearly, the executioner realised who was coming and was trying to make a quick job of it. As he was about to swing the axe, Hope dived at him taking the man to the ground, sending the axe clattering. Macleod saw another man go to pick it up and he ran into him, the pair of them tumbling across the floor. Hope was quick and had handcuffed her man, and was already up and on top of Macleod's assailant. She forced him to the ground, took his arm up behind his back, and then turned over to look at what Macleod was doing. The inspector, having recovered himself, was making his way back towards McGovern who should have been on the floor but instead, the man had lifted himself up. With his hands tied behind his back, he was now running from the large room they were in.

'Wait,' shouted Macleod, 'just wait. If you go, Devine will kill you. You can't be free of him.'

There was no response except for the sound of feet on cold stone making their way down the stairs.

Chapter 23

Macleod tore down the steps after McGovern, but the man was showing tremendous agility for someone who had just been tied up. Maybe the thought of an axe coming down on his neck had raised the stakes somewhat and driven him onto feats previously he would have thought twice about. As Macleod reached the bottom of the steps, he saw the door to the outside swinging on its hinges. Macleod stepped through and it opened onto the parking area at the far side of the building. There were a number of police officers standing in a makeshift cordon.

'Where did he go?' shouted Macleod at them.

'No one came out here, Inspector,' a voice shouted, and Macleod doubled back into the building again. He had come down the stairs and had gone straight through the swinging door which had led to the outside, but there was another door leading back into the building. Macleod opened this in a hurry, looking inside, but on seeing no one within that corridor, he made his way down, and opened another door to peer inside a further room. There was a blow to the back of his head and Macleod fell hard.

The world began to spin, and Macleod thought to get his hands up and over his head waiting for another blow but none came. Instead, he heard footsteps disappearing away from him, but the room was still swinging, and Macleod was struggling to get back up on his feet. For a moment, it seemed he couldn't do anything and then there was a voice beside him.

'Seoras, are you okay?'

Macleod managed to reach back and touch the rear of his head; bringing his hand to the front, he saw no blood. 'He clobbered me. He's gone that way. After him, Hope, go.'

It was a good three minutes later before Macleod had made his way back out of the building. His feet were a little unsteady and Hope was nowhere to be seen. Looking around, he could still see the police cordon, but then a black car suddenly came to life. Constables jumped into the cars to follow, and Macleod stumbled on out but eventually, he sat down on the bonnet of an empty police car the black car had sent spinning. A moment later, Hope came running out of the building.

'Where is he, Seoras? I've searched the whole thing. I can't find him.'

'He's gone,' said Macleod. 'Got in the car that took him and drove off. They're in pursuit.' Hope ran over to her boss holding him upright.

'It's just a knock, it will wear off in a minute.'

'No, it won't. Let's get you in the car.' As Hope helped Macleod back into their officer's car, Ross was on the phone keeping up with the chase.

'We need to get to Erin McGinty's now.'

Ross clambered into the front seat and once Hope was on board, he drove as fast as he could to the street Macleod had visited only a few days before. It appeared to be closed off, two police cars at one end, and Macleod stepped out unsteadily once Ross had parked up near them.

'What's going on, Constable?' asked Macleod.

'He's gone inside and McGinty's also inside. We did get some people to the door, but she screamed, told us to get back, said he was threatening her, possible gun.'

Macleod was feeling groggy. A blow to the back of the head had knocked him senseless, and every time he opened his eyes, Hope was in front of him staring back.

'You really need to step down, sir,' said Hope.

'No, what's going on?'

'He's holed up. He's got a hostage.'

'Have we asked for any other teams to come out?'

'Yes.'

'Okay,' said Macleod, 'just make sure we have surrounded the entire scene.'

It took a while, and more police cars turned up, but soon, the area was surrounded. Macleod was led away to an ambulance, but he noted that the DCI had turned up, clearly ready to take the glory of grabbing the man while Macleod was treated inside the ambulance.

The DCI gave him a tap on the shoulder, 'Good work, Macleod. I'll take it from here. Not to worry. You've done well.'

Macleod thought he had. McGovern was here, but something was still bothering the inspector. Erin McGinty was being threatened, but something was ticking away in the back of his mind. He sat in the back of the ambulance being checked over and saw a friendly face coming towards him.

'Why are you not up there?' asked Macleod. 'You should be finishing this off.'

'Well, the DCI is all over it, hostage situation. Don't need the murder team anymore,' said Hope. 'I've got Ross watching. I just wanted to make sure you were all right.'

'You've got a bad concussion,' said the ambulance driver. 'He's going to be out of action for a while.'

'The world's still spinning a bit,' said Macleod, 'it's not as bad as it was back in that warehouse, but it'll do.'

'At least we've got him trapped now. Do you think he did it?'

'I don't know what to think at the moment, Hope, and I'm not sure if it's me, my doubts, or just this bang to the head. Still, the DCI shouldn't be able to mess it up from here.'

'I've got Ross watching, just in case,' said Hope.

Macleod nodded and sat stretching back on the seat he had been forced into.

As he sat there, there was a shout from outside, and he went to get up from the chair but was restrained by the ambulance driver. 'Where are you going?'

'Hope, find out who that was.' She nodded and disappeared.

'But you're not going anywhere,' said the ambulance driver. 'You stay here, okay?' Macleod tried to relax, but something was bothering him, and there clearly seemed to be a commotion outside. He could hear people on the move. Hope was back with him two minutes later.

'Seems McGovern has done a runner. He's gone out of the back of the house, but we've got a full cordon out there.'

'He's trying to run. How did they know?'

'There was a shout, and McGinty said he'd gone out the back so everyone's closed in around that position.'

'When you say everyone, I take it we're still holding the cordon.'

'There's an officer or two.'

'One or two!' shouted Macleod. 'Get me up, I need to see this.'

'You're not going anywhere,' said the ambulance driver.

'Look, son, once this is done you can take me where you want, but right now I need to see this. Hope.'

The Inspector held out his arm and Hope pulled him up. Together they tumbled out of the ambulance onto the pavement. She walked Macleod forward, and he looked around. The cordon had indeed dispersed. There were only a couple of officers at the far end, one of whom then seemed to be sent further away. Macleod saw a figure he thought he recognised moving towards the house. As it approached the front door, it opened, and Macleod saw Devine entering the building.

'The house, Hope, McGovern's in the house. Run!'

Macleod tried to accelerate but every step was hard and he found himself having to concentrate just to get across the road towards the McGinty house. Hope was bounding ahead and he saw her entering the front door at the same time as he heard a terrible gunshot which caused a cascade of echoes in the street. Macleod continued to stumble forward into the house. He shouted out loud, 'McGrath, McGrath,' as he entered, praying that Hope was all right.

'Upstairs sir—need a hand,' she shouted.

It took an effort for him to climb up the stairs and as he reached the top, he heard the front door being pushed open again and more people entering the house. He stumbled onto the landing and then towards a bedroom door where Hope was standing. As he looked inside, he saw a picture of a man with a gun. Devine was laughing. Erin McGinty was on the far side of the room, blood on her clothing and there, lying in the most peculiar angle against the bed, was McGovern. There was a bloody wound in the stomach and a clean shot to the head. The man was clearly never going to get up again.

'Gun down,' said Macleod. 'It's over Devine, gun down. There's nowhere to go.'

'You're good, Inspector, you were very good. Every time you moved, one of your boys told me what was in your way, but I couldn't wait for you. Did you know that? I killed Fudge as well.'

'But why? He hadn't done anything. And what about this one?'

'This one. He took my woman; he blew up my star.'

Macleod was finding it hard to stand and had a fight holding himself up against the wall. 'Put the gun down, Devine.'

Macleod watched Devine place it on the floor and kick it over to Hope.

'Good,' said Macleod, 'Now, Hope, cuff him.'

With that, Macleod sat down on the floor, unable to continue to stand. The room was swimming again. He noted that Hope took the man out of the room, and then Erin McGinty was in his face, thanking him.

'He was going to kill me, but he said he wanted me. Was that what this was all about? He had an obsession for me. Thank you, Inspector, thank you.' Soon, the room went very dark.

Macleod woke up to the smiling face of Jane. 'Where am I, Love?'

'Raigmore Hospital. They said they're just going to watch you for a day or two. You and me are taking some time off. You need a short break. They said the concussion's not going to help either. You'll have to be away for a month or so from work, but you got him, as ever. You got your man, Seoras.'

Macleod lay back, his head on the pillow. His mind ached, struggling to comprehend how he had got here. But part of him wanted to get up because he believed the job was not yet finished.

Chapter 24

The next two weeks for Macleod involved check-ups at the hospital and the occasional piece of paperwork. Devine had been arrested, held for the murder of McGovern. It seemed that McGovern had decided to do a runner then come back inside the house once he'd realised the full extent of the cordon around the building. Devine had been let through the small cordon, by the very constable who had leaked him all the information.

Macleod was delighted that that man was getting the book thrown at him after Devine explained that he had been tipped off. McGovern, because of his infatuation with Erin McGinty, had been keen to move Eamon McGinty out of the way. In a stroke of genius, he planted the bomb rather than simply shooting him, making people think that there was a turf war going on. From there, things escalated. He'd been clever enough to feed everyone's fears by taking out Frank Egg, making out there had been a revenge attack.

His DNA was also found on Maggie Brown. It was said that he raped her before killing her, thus setting Devine off on his killing spree. During the interviews that followed, Devine showed no remorse. A man who, despite the fact that he had a wife and family, felt he had nothing, having lost Maggie Brown.

The DCI was happy despite the blunder of letting Devine in to kill their chief suspect in the case of the bombing, but everything was wrapped up and settling down. Of course, there'd be a proper trial, but Devine was pleading guilty and the bombing was attributed to McGovern.

There wasn't a lot left to do. Devine even admitted ordering the kill on Dermot Fudge. A time when Devine stated he was going crazy and just needed answers.

Macleod felt very aloof from all of this. With Jane's tender administrations, he had been relaxing, trying to let his head settle again. Erin McGinty was taking her kids and getting away from it all, telling Hope McGrath that she simply needed to be away. Her husband was dead, but at least she was getting clear of the lifestyle he'd been living and she felt safer. She would, of course, be back for the trial, but in the meantime, she advised she was on the up.

Macleod made it back into the office, simply for a visit, rather than to do any work. The team was delighted to see him. He chatted, had coffee, and took a scan over some rather unremarkable cases they were looking into. Before returning home, Hope said she didn't want to see him for another couple of weeks. She was on top of it anyway and there was no need for the old man to be in. He agreed but checked Hope's statement from Erin McGinty one more time before departing.

That night at home, Macleod had been looking up many different holiday destinations, but one struck him, and he turned to Jane. 'How do you fancy going to Mexico? We could take a week, maybe two.'

'Mexico? I'd love to. What are you going to do in Mexico?'

'I just wish to get a little sun, somewhere quiet, sitting on the beach.'

'You don't like the beach,' said Jane. 'Why are you going to the beach?'

'I need to rest. You like the beach. You have to force me to rest, get this head back where it should be.'

'We can go to Mexico,' said Jane, 'but I think your head's already where it should be.' Macleod gave her a devious stare, but he knew she was on to something.

Macleod managed to get plane tickets out, and they flew to Mexico two days later. At first, they travelled to La Paz, before Macleod said he wanted to see the south of Baja California, and in a hire car, he drove all the way down to Cabo San Lucas. There in San Lucas, they managed to take up a small flat, and for a week, Macleod sat every day on the beach, on the pedregal plain, letting himself soak in the sun.

Beside him, Jane would pour sun cream on him, on herself, and together, they'd bake. The evenings were taken up with meals and short walks, and the only thing Jane had queried was what Seoras was really doing.

It was on a Tuesday, around 11:00 a.m., after lying on the beach, that Seoras stood up, looked down at Jane, and told her that he was going for a short walk.

'And this is why we're here,' she said.

Macleod smiled. 'Sorry, I have to do this.'

'I know,' she said. 'I don't know what it is, but I know you have to do it, but I've got a free holiday from it, and I've got you to myself, after this next what, hour? So, go do it, Seoras. And when you're done, come back here, and lie down beside me.'

The sand was immaculate, lying before an ocean of blue.

There were little rocks, but Macleod strode towards some palm trees that led up to a number of houses and flats that reminded him of the 1970s. Every building seemed flat, but elongated, with the only tilted roofs being those of courtyards that were open. Otherwise, every roof seemed to be flat. Macleod made his way up the street that wound up the hill, and he recognised several places he'd walked past three days before. At the corner of one house, he stopped and saw a swimming pool at the rear.

There were two children playing, laughing as they threw water at each other, and then a small woman was there in a bikini. Macleod had only ever seen her inside her house, apparently agitated by the death of her husband. As he started to walk up the drive towards the house, he realised she looked a lot less tense. Macleod rang the doorbell and waited until Erin McGinty appeared from the side of the house.

'Detective Inspector, what are you doing here?

'Well, you weren't going to come back to Scotland, were you? One of my sergeants said you were heading south, started to make sense. I might have been able to stop you but McGovern gave me a heck of a crack on the head and left my head swimming. Two weeks I couldn't piece together anything. Then I thought I knew what was going on but I can't prove it and I can't do anything about it.'

'This sounds bad, Inspector. Why are you here in Mexico? Do you mind if we sit somewhere? Around the back.'

Macleod made his way to the side of the house looking inside through any window at the quite stunning furnishings. 'You've done all right for yourself, haven't you? But then again, Eamon must have money put aside somewhere. Nice of him to. Maybe he did love you in his own way.'

Macleod caught a glimpse of anger from McGinty but she

asked him to take a seat before disappearing inside the house and coming out with a pot of tea. 'Some things you bring with you, don't you?' she said to Macleod. 'But I'm afraid the milk's rubbish. You'll have to drink it black.'

Macleod didn't want tea anyway, and it would probably sit there in front of him but he nodded. 'You were very clever.'

'Was I?' said Erin McGinty.

'Very. You realised the infatuation of McGovern. That's when you were able to actually plan. There was a cost there, wasn't there? McGovern didn't come for cheap.'

'You seem to know a lot, Inspector; why don't you continue?'

'You whored for McGovern and he was the one who got hold of the Semtex. He was the one who used Devine's name. He was the one who brought it, but you were the one who planted it. You see, McGovern, a nasty piece of work, but blowing up a coach load of people... It didn't sit with me, blowing up a coach load of people just to get a husband. He would have had an opportunity within the firm. He could have made it look like normal gang business, if it were his idea, he could have involved Declan O'Malley's gang in a much stronger way but, no. A bomb right under the seat where he was sitting.

'Who knew where your husband would be going that day? He was a careful man. He had to be doing what he did. You said to me he told you things. You understood a lot because you were his confidant, as much as you didn't like him and what he did, as much as he treated you roughly, you were still the one he told.

'You knew he'd be on the coach; therefore, you planted the bomb and you killed him but you made it look like a turf war. McGovern was quite happy to take out Frank Egg. I guess the two of you must have done that one. Bit of work to lift him up.

I don't know if McGovern got other people involved, called that revenge attack. Tit for tat or Devine said to do it. Half the people in these organisations don't really know who says what. It's just fed down, easy to do. Then you take out Devine's girl.

'That's a stroke of genius and McGovern does it because he doesn't like Devine either and he likes the rough stuff. That's why his DNA's on her. But the two of you killed her, bringing Devine into it and Devine goes after one of them at that point. Declan O'Malley doesn't play ball but it doesn't matter because you've set Devine off and then he's killing Fudge; he's coming for anyone. That's the bit that McGovern was dumb about. He didn't understand that as soon as the tale about the Semtex was out from us, he was a dead man. Lucky break that one, stopped you having to dispose of McGovern. But I reckon you had a back-up plan to dispose of him anyway.

'Nobody should have known who got the Semtex, Inspector, but your tell-tale worked a treat.'

'It nearly backfired on you though, didn't it? McGovern was meant to come round to yours anyway and you would then call Devine. Devine was going to come round and kill him but McGovern got spotted because I'm not that slack. If a man's on the loose, I'll find him. Then I got hit on the head because Devine wouldn't have gotten in that house with me being there. He got lucky but in truth for the rest of it, in a purely professional capacity, Mrs McGinty, I am impressed. I am impressed because while I know all these things, I can prove none of them. Tell me, did Eamon teach you how to clean up a crime scene?'

'You don't become the wife of someone like that and not have to do some of the dirty work at some point, Inspector,' smiled Erin McGinty. 'The thing is I didn't want it, but he involved me, so I let him teach me how to do these things. I let him and because of that, I knew how I could plan his death, how to make it look like there was a gang war kicking it off.

'As I said, in a professional sense, I'm impressed,' said Macleod. 'But understand this, you took over thirty people to their grave just to be here. What sickens me is you don't even have a conscience about that.'

'I have had plenty happen to me, and a little rain must fall into every life. I'd like to tell you it wasn't worth it, Inspector, but it was. Look at me, look at them.' She pointed at the kids splashing in the pool.

'Oh, forgive me,' said Macleod, rising. 'I hope you choke in all this. I know I can't prove what you've done, and professionally for me, that's all right because you see, there's always one that gets away, even if you know how they did it.'

'I bet it eats at you, Inspector,' said Erin McGinty, 'I bet you it eats at you.'

Macleod stood up. 'I'm not accustomed to being in shorts.' He stared down at his feet, looking at the sandals and socks he had on. He turned back to the woman. 'What you don't get, is I don't do this because I need justice to be served. It will be one far greater than I. No, I'll go on and my conscience will be fine but one day, you'll be called to reckon, and I hope you see the light before then.' Macleod walked down the drive, hearing the jeers of Erin McGinty behind him, shouting at him how it would be a champagne breakfast for her.

He didn't look back but continued back to the beach where he saw Jane continuing to sunbathe. When he reached his partner, he sat down and laid back beside her.

'Well done, love,' said Jane. 'Well done. But tell me, will you be making a habit of this?'

205

'Of what?' asked Macleod.

'Chasing your criminals to foreign parts.'

'No,' said Macleod.

'Pity.'

'Pity?' queried Macleod. 'Why?'

'I've got a list of destinations you might think of trying.'

Read on to discover the Patrick Smythe series!

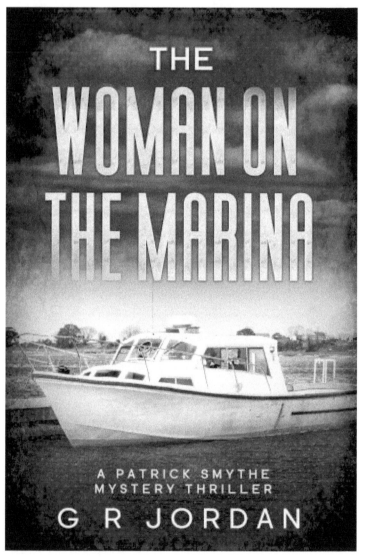

Start your Patrick Smythe journey here!

Patrick Smythe is a former Northern Irish policeman who

after suffering an amputation after a bomb blast, takes to the sea between the west coast of Scotland and his homeland to ply his trade as a private investigator. Join Paddy as he tries to work to his own ethics while knowing how to bend the rules he once enforced. Working from his beloved motorboat 'Craigantlet', Paddy decides to rescue a drug mule in this short story from the pen of G R Jordan.

Join G R Jordan's monthly newsletter about forthcoming releases and special writings for his tribe of avid readers and then receive your free Patrick Smythe short story.

Go to https://bit.ly/PatrickSmythe for your Patrick Smythe journey to start!

About the Author

GR Jordan is a self-published author who finally decided at forty that in order to have an enjoyable lifestyle, his creative beast within would have to be unleashed. His books mirror that conflict in life where acts of decency contend with self-promotion, goodness stares in horror at evil, and kindness blindsides us when we at our worst. Corrupting our world with his parade of wondrous and horrific characters, he highlights everyday tensions with fresh eyes whilst taking his methodical, intelligent mainstays on a roller-coaster ride of dilemmas, all the while suffering the banter of their provocative sidekicks.

A graduate of Loughborough University where he masqueraded as a chemical engineer but ultimately played American football, Gary had worked at changing the shape of cereal flakes and pulled a pallet truck for a living. Watching vegetables freeze at -40'C was another career highlight and he was also one of the Scottish Highlands "blind" air traffic controllers.

These days he has graduated to answering a telephone to people in trouble before telephoning other people to sort it out.

Having flirted with most places in the UK, he is now based in the Isle of Lewis in Scotland where his free time is spent between raising a young family with his wife, writing, figuring out how to work a loom and caring for a small flock of chickens. Luckily, his writing is influenced by his varied work and life experience as the chickens have not been the poetical inspiration he had hoped for!

You can connect with me on:
🌐 https://grjordan.com
📘 https://facebook.com/carpetlessleprechaun

Subscribe to my newsletter:
✉ https://bit.ly/PatrickSmythe

Also by G R Jordan

G R Jordan writes across multiple genres including crime, dark and action adventure fantasy, feel good fantasy, mystery thriller and horror fantasy. Below is a selection of his work. Whilst all books are available across online stores, signed copies are available at his personal shop.

The Culling at Singing Sands (Highlands & Islands Detective Book 15)
https://grjordan.com/product/the-culling-at-singing-sands
A glamorous retirement village on an isolated island. A brutal killer culls the elderly starting with the oldest resident. Can Macleod discover the murderous motive and prevent the island graveyard from overflowing?

When the Isle of Eigg enjoys the opening of 'The Singing Sands' Later but Better Township', little do they realise that death is only round the corner for the new arrivals. Joy turns to sorrow as old friends meet a bloody end, and DI Macleod and DS McGrath are dispatched to investigate. As a determined clientele and some unseasonal weather hamper the investigation, the detectives must look to the past to prevent the dispatching of those seen to be past their time.

Even in paradise you're only one step from the grave!

The Hunted Child (Kirsten Stewart Thrillers #2)

https://grjordan.com/product/the-hunted-child

A twelve-year-old witness to a drug killing goes on the run. The murderer puts a price on the child's head. Can Kirsten Stewart pick up the girl's trail, or will she meet a bloody end from the pursuing bounty hunters?

When a young girl inadvertently stumbles upon a drug gang execution, she sets in motion a brutal hunt like the Highlands has never seen. From farmland to coast, mountain to valley, no hiding place will bring a safe haven. But when Service operative Kirsten Stewart picks up the trail, she realises there's more than one hand in play.

In her second solo novel, Kirsten has to rely heavily on her own instincts as she finds the shadowy world she now operates in becoming darker still. With the pressure of a child's life in the balance, Kirsten has to draw on all her mental and physical resources, if she is to stop an innocent girl falling to a killer's knife.

The bloody scramble for the innocent has begun...

Corpse Reviver (A Contessa Munroe Mystery #1)
https://grjordan.com/product/corspe-reviver

A widowed Contessa flees to the northern waters in search of adventure. An entrepreneur dies on an ice pack excursion. But when the victim starts moonlighting from his locked cabin, can the Contessa uncover the true mystery of his death?

Catriona Cullodena Munroe, widow of the late Count de Los Palermo, has fled the family home, avoiding the scramble for title and land. As she searches for the life she always wanted, the Contessa, in the company of the autistic and rejected Tiff, must solve the mystery of a man who just won't let his business go.

Corpse Reviver is the first murder mystery involving the formidable and sometimes downright rude lady of leisure and her straight talking niece. Bonded by blood, and thrown together by fate, join this pair of thrill seekers as they realise that flirting with danger brings a price to pay.

Highlands and Islands Detective Thriller Series
https://grjordan.com/product/waters-edge

Join stalwart DI Macleod and his burgeoning new DC McGrath as they look into the darker side of the stunningly scenic and wilder parts of the north of Scotland. From the Black Isle to Lewis, from Mull to Harris and across to the small Isles, the Uists and Barra, this mismatched pairing follow murders, thieves and vengeful victims in an effort to restore tranquillity to the remoter parts of the land.

Be part of this tale of a surprise partnership amidst the foulest deeds and darkest souls who stalk this peaceful and most beautiful of lands, and you'll never see the Highlands the same way again

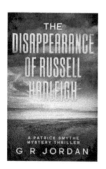

The Disappearance of Russell Hadleigh (Patrick Smythe Book 1)

https://grjordan.com/product/the-disappearance-of-russell-hadleigh

A retired judge fails to meet his golf partner. His wife calls for help while running a fantasy play ring. When Russians start co-opting into a fairly-traded clothing brand, can Paddy untangle the strands before the bodies start littering the golf course?

In his first full novel, Patrick Smythe, the single-armed former policeman, must infiltrate the golfing social scene to discover the fate of his client's husband. Assisted by a young starlet of the greens, Paddy tries to understand just who bears a grudge and who likes to play in the rough, culminating in a high stakes showdown where lives are hanging by the reaction of a moment. If you love pacey action, suspicious motives and devious characters, then Paddy Smythe operates amongst your kind of people.

Love is a matter of taste but money always demands more of its suitor.

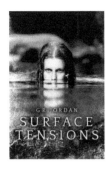

Surface Tensions (Island Adventures Book 1)
https://grjordan.com/product/surface-tensions
Mermaids sighted near a Scottish island. A town exploding in anger and distrust. And Donald's got to get the sexiest fish in town, back in the water.

"Surface Tensions" is the first story in a series of Island adventures from the pen of G R Jordan. If you love comic moments, cosy adventures and light fantasy action, then you'll love these tales with a twist. Get the book that amazon readers said, "perfectly captures life in the Scottish Hebrides" and that explores "human nature at its best and worst".

Something's stirring the water!

Lightning Source UK Ltd.
Milton Keynes UK
UKHW021451211022
410863UK00001B/193

9 781914 073526